Other Available Books by Sherry Lynn Ferguson:

Lord Sidley's Last Season
Quiet Meg
The Honorable Marksley

MAJOR
LORD DAVID

•

Sherry Lynn
Ferguson

AVALON BOOKS
NEW YORK

Published by Avalon Books, an imprint of
Thomas Bouregy & Co., Inc.
160 Madison Avenue, New York, NY 10016

Library of Congress Cataloging-in-Publication Data

Ferguson, Sherry Lynn.
Major Lord David / Sherry Lynn Ferguson.
p. cm.
ISBN 978-0-8034-7786-5 (hardcover)
1. Aristocracy (Social class)—England—Fiction.
I. Title.
PS3606.E727M35 2010
813'.6—dc22

2010016363

PRINTED IN THE UNITED STATES OF AMERICA
ON ACID-FREE PAPER
BY HADDON CRAFTSMEN, BLOOMSBURG, PENNSYLVANIA

For B, who loves history—and makes it

Chapter One

The year 1815 was at the door, but the Duke of Braughton's guests refused to admit it. The crowd's easy laughter and excited conversation continued unabated as midnight and the first of January approached.

Observing the revelers, David found nothing lacking. This New Year's celebration was one of a long line of happy gatherings. For more than three decades his parents had entertained family, friends, and neighbors in grand fashion at the castle—the massive, medieval "ruin," as his brother, Myles, Marquis of Hayden, inevitably referred to their eminence of a home. Tonight Braughton overflowed with greenery, candles, mirrors, and colorful swags, and sheltered a throng of masked visitors. Their joyful activity warmed the lofty Leicestershire halls, turning the place into what Hayden had also ruefully termed an "inn."

Hayden was heir to it all. He might call it what he chose. Yet David reflected that few inns could boast Braughton's extensive number of beautifully appointed guest suites.

Just now the festive ballroom was a spectacle indeed—such a melding of motion, music, and merry anticipation that any observer's heart would have instantly lightened. For David, who had missed the occasion for far too many years, the sight was doubly welcome.

He knew the duke and duchess celebrated not only the holiday but his own return from Paris. He also knew that his parents intended that this time the homecoming be permanent. To be home was his desire as well; it had been his dearest goal for six long years. He had held this vision of Braughton in dreams, on every tedious march, through every campaign, for all the years of war on the Peninsula. Its realization had been delayed last fall, when his colonel had recommended unexpectedly that he accompany Wellington and the occupying allied forces to Paris. But the terms of his return here to Leicestershire were the sticking point, for his father was suggesting, however discreetly, that his second son, Lord David, should be thinking of marriage. And the duke had gone so far as to select, most efficiently and carefully, the bride.

David sighed as he stood pensively at Hayden's side. In keeping with the spirit of the evening, his brother had donned an elaborate mask, one that covered his eyes and extended on either side of his face into gilded rays—portraying the sun, perhaps, or possibly the mane of a lion. Either role would have suited him. Despite the mask Hayden was unmistakable, given his distinctive flaxen hair, his tall form, and his immaculate clothing. In town, some wags even called Hayden "His Resplendence."

"I never tire of looking at that man," one masked lady whispered as she and a gaping companion passed in front of their post. David knew the two women referred to Hayden. Yet his brother appeared oblivious, his attention fixed on the opposite side of the ballroom, where a lively country dance had just commenced.

"And what draws your interest so, Myles?" David asked. They were of a height, such that when the mask turned to him, David met the hooded look in Hayden's level blue gaze.

"Love," he said, and his lips rose in a grin. He nodded toward their cousin Charles Cabot and his new wife.

"Chas and Meg," David agreed. "Yes." Though the pair now stood apart in the midst of the dance, their attachment was palpable. Yet they had come alarmingly close to losing their future together—and their very lives.

"A good job, that, David," Hayden remarked. "Chas might have died but for your care."

David shook his head. "He could not have died, knowing Meg awaited him." He followed the two in the energetic figures of the dance. "No wonder Chas smiles so. Were I similarly blessed, I'd want the world to know it. Watching them is a pleasure, gratifying to us all. I'm happy for them."

Hayden stared at him. "You're fickle, David."

"Why so? I met Meg Lawrence on her wedding day. She's now as close as we shall ever come to having a sister. And I'm a practical man, Myles. I would never have had a chance with her."

"Well, you see, that is where I must wonder." Hayden paused. Behind the mask his expression was indecipherable. " 'Twould not have been a bad match," he mused aloud.

"That you say so tells me it would have been far from *good*. You are too cynical, Myles. I'll wager someday you'll regret it." David pointedly looked back at the dancers. "You could not have made Meg as happy."

"Oh, I know *that*. That is one of the regrets. But happiness is your standard, is it?"

"Unless one is a completely selfish beast." Again he looked to his brother's hidden eyes, so strangely mirroring his own. "Why did you not take a chance with her, then? You'd seen Meg Lawrence years before Chas ever met her."

"I believed her taken—another's property. And I was slow to consider it. Complacent, I 'spose. *Grand-mère* would call me worse. I hadn't Chas' pluck."

David sighed once more. "Perhaps it was not quite right, else you would have tried."

"I suspect 'twill never be 'quite right.' " Hayden attempted to ease the mask upon his nose. "Yet I must marry this year. I must settle. I shall be thirty-two."

David laughed. "Is it a prescription, then? Heaven forbid that you should ever let your heart rule your head."

With a dismissive sound, Hayden returned to reviewing the ballroom.

"Has Father been after you as well?" David pressed. He wondered if their father's plans extended to matrimony for both of them.

"Not at all."

David considered that as he also surveyed the merrymakers. "You frighten me sometimes, Myles," he commented at last. "I wonder if there is a woman in the world who might trump your sense of duty."

Hayden answered only with silence. Again David found his own attention caught by the slim, shapely woman dressed as a Spanish *señorita* in colorful, tiered, ruffled skirts and a lacy mantilla with combs. But the mantilla could not entirely cover her lustrous chestnut hair, nor could her black domino hide a creamy complexion and delicately bowed lips. David had tracked her much of the past hour. He'd noticed her walk. It was perhaps the least self-conscious walk he had ever seen in a woman—modest, yet light and free, with nothing of feminine feints or flirtation. Because of the *señorita*'s presence at the ball, David had been looking forward with considerable expectation to midnight's unmasking.

"Speakin' of duty," Hayden said, breaking in upon his reverie. "Have you spoken to our neighbor Caswell yet?"

"No." David's high spirits immediately plunged. "Why should it be my task, when *he* seeks the interview? Father might present me at any time. I've seen him over there, with Caswell and two of his sons and half a dozen other neighbors. If they wish to acquaint me with the girl, let them get on with it. I've not been hiding. Meantime, this is my home— and a holiday."

"Indeed, little brother. And you have a certain role—as a host."

"I've been about it! I've danced with every matron in the place and not touched a drop of anything stronger than the punch. If I want a trot with the chestnut filly before confronting Sir Moreton Caswell, what's wrong with that?"

Hayden shrugged and looked at the *señorita*. "Do you know who she is?" he asked.

"I expected you to tell me that."

"You assume I know everybody in the place, even masked?"

"Quite frankly, yes. You are usually *au fait* with most matters, Lord Hayden. But I believe I might wait for midnight's revelations. It wants only twenty minutes to the hour."

Hayden sighed. "Deuced uncomfortable," he muttered, pushing the mask an increment higher above his nose.

"You might have dispensed with the contraption. Everyone knows perfectly well who you are. Chas certainly did not bother, and I knew my regimentals would betray me."

"More than your regimentals, perhaps, Major. But unlike you, I am sharing in the spirit of the occasion."

David laughed. "*Mon frère,* you are unexpectedly agreeable. *Grand-mère* will suspect you have been tamed. 'Without teeth!' *Le marquis sans dents! Le marquis manqué!*"

People turned to look at him. He'd been told he had a pleasant laugh. Yet David was not aware of laughing all that often—certainly not during the past few years. He supposed the compliment was meant to encourage him, like commending the smile of a shy wallflower.

His laugh attracted the attention of another bystander. Masked Squire Melrose, singular in his stoutness, sidled up to David's side. "Lord David!" he boomed. "Will you be treating us to a song tonight?"

"I had not planned on it tonight, Squire." David nodded politely. "I have not had enough punch."

"Not enough punch? Well! That is soon remedied, surely? I shall bring you a cup." As Melrose trundled off in the direction of the refreshments, Hayden groaned.

"Now you are in for it. Are you in good voice, or must we tolerate the usual?"

"Your support and encouragement are always so welcome, Myles," David commented dryly.

"Compliments are not my function."

"Oh? What is?"

Hayden shrugged. "I am your brother."

David silently wondered just what filial obligations Lord Hayden deigned to acknowledge. But as for singing—perhaps singing would not be *that* bad. Many years ago, David used to sing frequently.

"I shall sing if pressed," he conceded. "Since you reprimand me, I shall attempt to participate in the *esprit de parti.*"

Hayden grinned at him and nodded in the direction of the dancing *señorita.*

"You might skip over now to ask the lady, before you are forced to yodel. Granted, she is a bonny bit. But what in particular appeals to you?"

"In particular? I believe she reminds me of Mateo."

"Mateo? Your *horse*? The one you lost at Salamanca?"

"The same," he admitted, smiling. "He was a beautiful chestnut."

"I thought I needn't school you in your approach, David. But as you liken the lady to a horse, perhaps I must. 'Twould at least justify spending such a sobering amount of time on New Year's Eve speakin' to my own brother!"

"I beg your forbearance, Hayden. Though I must admit I've enjoyed our limited exchanges these past six years."

"Indeed." He bowed deeply. "My pleasure, my lord."

"Mine, my lord." David returned the bow and watched Hayden stroll off to a knot of guests. They had always amused each other; David trusted his own affection was returned. But like their father the duke, Lord Hayden revealed little of his feelings. Their *grand-mère* claimed that Hayden grew colder— a claim David had disputed. But the heir to Braughton was unmistakably reserved.

The dance set was ending. The *señorita* had come closer.

Proximity only enhanced her attractions. Through the last strains of music and the laughter and chatter, David could hear the great clock in the hall strike the three-quarter hour. With reckless resignation, he moved toward the amber-haired beauty. He thought, with a certain practicality, that he must satisfy the urge to dance with her—or be forced to sing.

The *señorita* was fanning her flushed cheeks while speaking to her partner, young Frank Farrington, the vicar's son. Though Farrington had also disguised much of his face, his skinny neck and prominent Adam's apple betrayed him. David bowed before focusing entirely on the lady. Her black satin mask frustrated him. Her eyes looked dark and long-lashed, but he could only guess at their color. Everything else about her was perfection.

"*Señorita, me permite*—may I have this next dance?"

"Oh! My lord . . . Major . . ." Her voice was sweet. She was surprised. "I regret—that is, this gentleman . . ."

Farrington had the good grace to yield. "I would not keep you, miss, from the guest of honor," he said, and he nodded to David. "My lord."

David offered the girl his arm, noting with satisfaction that the *señorita*'s fingers held no wedding ring. And she was tall—her face was close, closer than he'd anticipated. He had to concentrate on taking a place in the set as the orchestra struck the opening chords. Near to, her hair looked like streaming silk, the color of rich caramel.

"*Querida,*" he said, as they passed in the dance. "*Nos conocemos.* We have met before."

"You know me?" Again she was surprised. And her anxiety intrigued him, for despite the masks, this house party consisted of few who were unknown to one another, though David had been away long enough that many were now less than familiar to him.

"I meant only that you and I were never intended to be strangers," he reassured her.

"We are not strangers."

"No," he agreed, smiling. "We are of one mind."

He thought she was also tempted to smile.

"You have met me before, Major—Lord David."

"Never! I can only ever have paid you the most minute attention. I should have remembered. And my memory has never been faulted."

" 'Twas some time ago. I have known you and your brother many years."

"Hayden too, then? I am not certain it is such a recommendation that you know Hayden." With a quick, unreasoning jealousy, he wondered how well Myles could know this beauty; he certainly had not let on. In the dance David let his hand skim her arm lightly and too forwardly.

She moved away.

"I see your cousin, Charles Cabot," she said.

"You know Chas as well?"

"Of course. He used to live here at Braughton for a time. I remember him riding a huge white horse named Falstaff."

David almost missed a step. "You must have been very young! Falstaff has been dead these eight years!"

The *señorita* bit her luscious lower lip. "The lady with Charles tonight . . . is very lovely. Even with the mask, she is . . . she is . . ."

"Indescribable. Yes, that's Meg. Only someone as exceptional as Chas could do her justice—in any sense. Someday perhaps I shall tell you their story. Her father is Sir Eustace Lawrence, the barrister. Have you heard of him?"

She shook her head. "I've not been much in the world these four years, my lord."

"And why is that?" he asked softly, again bringing her arm close against his in the dance. "Have you just escaped from the seraglio? Or have you been held, like Rapunzel, in some distant tower?"

She smiled even as he led her, slowly and carefully, away

from the end of the line of dancers, toward a curtained alcove at the room's edge. As a son of the house, David knew every secret spot. And he intended to touch one of those irresistibly silky curls of dark chestnut hair.

"You must tell me," he said, drawing her gently into the shadowed window embrasure, "how you can know Hayden and yet not be much in the world. The two states would, to my mind, be mutually exclusive."

"I know him from here at Braughton, not from London. Just as I know you and your cousin Charles."

"Then you are not one of Hayden's . . . friends?"

Again she drew a sharp breath. "I have been away at *school,* my lord. You are hard on me—and on him."

"Forgive me. Hayden and I are used to teasing each other. You must not consider it cruel."

"He has always looked out for you."

"And you are his defender! *Querida,* you must tell me why you think Hayden cares one jot for me." She was permitting him to hold her—lightly, it was true, but hold her nonetheless. In their private enclave, an ancient ogee of arched stone screened them from the rest of the party.

"Why, I remember that time at the weir—" She broke off abruptly. And David knew he must look shocked. She could not know about the weir; only Myles and Chas knew of that incident, so many years ago, when Myles had risked much to save him from drowning.

As he frowned, he felt her slight attempt to withdraw, but the effort lacked will. His clasp on her was not tight; she might have fled him had she wished. But he did not intend to let the mystery elude him.

"Hayden told you about the weir," he suggested softly.

"I believe the dance is ending, my lord. We should—we should return." Just then she seemed to notice their distance from the company. But she worried her lips, which she should not have done.

"I wonder what might have prompted Hayden to relay the tale. In general he does not boast of heroics. No doubt"—David leaned closer—"he yielded to your considerable charms."

"It was not at all as you suppose! Ah . . ." Her attention had flickered beyond him. "How beautiful! 'Tis snowing. . . ." At the mullioned window a gust of snowflakes eddied in the dark, patting at the panes, obscuring the already snow-dusted spruce trees beyond. The dance had closed; the dancers were dispersing to refresh themselves. The orchestra had started to play Praetorius' tune, in anticipation of the New Year.

David knew the signals by heart. Braughton, both the duke and the legacy, had always introduced the New Year with this overture, and as Braughton had always done, so it would always do. But David would not release the *señorita*. Despite his awareness of the noise echoing in the high-ceilinged hall and the frolicking crowd so close to them, he felt curiously still, as though she and he were trapped together, muffled by snow. The rest of the world could only be a distraction.

"This music—it is a Christmas carol," she said, unwisely drawing his attention again to her lips.

" 'Tis my *grand-mère*'s favorite," he explained. "My father has it played for her every year, just before the turning of the new. Just now," he breathed, "it is apt." And he sang, very low, and for her ears alone:

> *"There bloomed a lovely flower*
> *Though winter's cold was blowing,*
> *And midnight—was the hour."*

His fingers captured one bright, luxurious lock of her hair. She did not pull away. For an instant her face was close enough that her breath mingled with his. Then the horns and clapping and cheers announced 1815.

"Querida," he murmured against her ear. "I believe you owe

me your name." Flattering as it was that her masked eyes were closed, David pulled away to observe her. And just in time.

"David!"

That was his father, with every ounce of reproach he could command—which, for His Grace of Braughton, was considerable. David turned to find his father flanked by an amused, unmasked Hayden and a furious Sir Moreton Caswell, Baronet.

"Wilhelmina Caswell!" Sir Moreton hissed. "*This* is how you choose to behave?" Thankfully, the man kept his voice low, though he was rapidly turning purple. David felt the girl's arm tremble in his grasp.

"Papa . . ." she said.

And David quickly withdrew his hold. He had to comprehend. *This,* the lovely *señorita,* was his neighbor, Caswell's daughter? The girl his father had been scheming for months for him to meet and marry?

"Sir—" he tried.

"Oh, this is too much!" Sir Moreton snapped. "Four years of fine schooling, Billie, and you must still . . ."

But David no longer heard Sir Moreton's fuming. His mind had seized upon the name *Billie.* Surely not the "Billie" Caswell who'd plagued him for years? The youngster who'd hounded him, tortured him, *injured* him, and interfered in every conceivable way with his pleasures at home? The "Billie" Caswell whom he'd believed just another of his neighbor's troop of *boys?*

He stepped back from her.

"Billie Caswell!" he charged, careless of the company. "Infuriating infant! My shoulder still aches in the cold! What a shock it must have been for you—to find yourself a *girl!*" He snatched the mask from her face. But the shock was his. For the *señorita* was even lovelier than he'd supposed. And the look in her eyes was an unforgiving blaze.

Chapter Two

Her brothers had whisked her away. In the midst of Braughton's revelry they had hurried her, looking white as the snow outside, out of the ballroom and far from him. Immediately David had done what he had to do, the only honorable thing to do; he had turned to Sir Moreton Caswell and apologized. He had requested to pay his addresses. He had, in essence, offered for her.

Caswell had muttered unintelligibly, but he had not said no, and David's father, the implacable Duke of Braughton, had said nothing at all.

After tentative, disheartened efforts to rejoin the celebrations, David had retired as well, and, like any practiced soldier, he had slept.

But as he stood staring at the next morning's bountiful breakfast buffet, and feeling as he now almost always felt at mealtimes—ravenous—he knew he deliberately avoided contemplating the previous night's happenings. He did not know whether he was promised or not; he did not know whether he was to be married. He could only hope that the rest of the year would not continue as it had begun.

There were too many people in the house. Despite the early hour there were too many people, easily forty or more, packed here in the breakfast room, and they were all still too happy. In the usual course, he would have enjoyed the company. But as he filled his plate, he wished he were not required to be sociable.

He'd noticed at least one of the Caswell brothers at the table—the eldest, priggish "Morty," who had sent him several baleful glances—but there was no sign of *her.*

Myles came to stand next to him at the sideboard. David glanced at him with some temper, heightened by the sight of that easy smile.

"You bounder," he said. "You *knew.*"

Myles' smile fled. "I did not know." For a moment he plucked with tongs at the sausages, then abandoned the sport and turned to him. "*Wilhelmina* Caswell and I have never been introduced. You have my word on it. The only failing I *will* claim, David, is my distraction last night, when I might have observed your *señorita*'s company. Though why I should have assumed that responsibility, given your own close reconnaissance, eludes me." He shrugged. "You yielded to an inclination, and duty binds you nonetheless. Need I say that is usually the way of things? 'Tis deplorable, blaming others when your own choices cause the constraints. I'd presumed you a better officer." And after that—one of the longer speeches David had heard from him in many years—the imperturbable Marquis of Hayden turned and abruptly left the room.

David noticed *Grand-mère*—his father's mother, the elderly Dowager Duchess of Braughton—at the far end of the table. Her presence surprised him, as she was not usually an early riser, until he observed that she still wore the previous night's ball gown. She had not even been to bed. That explained all; his inexhaustible French relative was a phenomenon indeed.

He walked the length of the table to take a seat next to her.

"*Mon pauvre*"—she spoke with some excitement—"what was it you said to him?"

David shrugged. "*Il se fâche,*" he said of Hayden.

"*Oui.* I see. He is indeed cross. Very good, David. Very good." But she examined his face with concern. "You must be brave, *mon enfant,* for this will take some time."

What did she mean by "this"? He was frowning when his cousin Chas placed a hand on his left shoulder and, leaning over, spoke in his ear.

"You must think of the girl," he advised, and for a second Chas' grave brown gaze met his own. Then Chas patted his shoulder and moved on.

At least his *grand-mère* and Chas had not disowned him. But they had always been the most sensible members of the family.

David stabbed his eggs.

"That is a sizable portion you have there, Major." Smug Morty Caswell was watching from across the table, with an annoyingly superior tilt to his chin.

"Had you starved in the Pyrenees, Caswell," David responded lightly, "you would not remark it."

As Morty Caswell turned pink, that end of the table fell silent. David heard his *grand-mère*'s "tsk," but he continued to eat undisturbed. In a moment the irrepressible spirits of the New Year had reasserted themselves, and the lively conversation resumed.

"That was not well done, *mon petit.*" His grandmother eyed him. "You forget you are a gentleman."

"It is possible to be too much the gentleman."

"Never! *Ce n'est pas possible!*"

"Hayden is your model, then, *Grand-mère,* is he?"

"The model is for everyone the same—to be genteel, to be kind! *C'est tout!* And though your brother is all that is proper, David, *you* are more often the 'model.' To be kind takes the warm heart."

He looked at her then, so tiny and silver-haired, and felt the reproach. "How did such a pretty young one as you are grow to be so wise?"

She smiled with that hint of shared confidence that had charmed so many. "I have the example of my grandsons," she replied diplomatically, "who are gentlemen."

He laughed, a sound that seemed to reassure the others at the table that Major Lord David Trent was not mad. His *grand-mère* shook her head.

"You look most like him, David. Like your *grand-père.* When you smile so—*eh, bien!*—I am again eighteen. So I must feel for this *jeune fille.* With *les premières amours.*"

"*Les premières amours? Que veut dire—?*"

"Oh, you know very well what I mean, else this *Duc de Fer* Wellington would not have wished you in Paris last fall!"

" 'Puppy love' is hardly a term old Hooky would use. And in any event it scarcely applies. There is no 'love' involved. This is simply a case of two meddling old men."

"So? I believe you wrong. But this 'puppy love'—it will pass. You need only wait."

For some reason he did not welcome the thought. David finished the rest of his breakfast in silence and tried not to think of himself as a soldier, at the disposal of others. Unfortunately, he found his status affirmed when he at last exited the dining room. He met his father and Sir Moreton Caswell heading into breakfast.

The Duke of Braughton, tall, stern, and well-used to exercising authority, did not trouble to wish his son a happy New Year.

"You will, of course, accompany the Caswells on their journey home today, David."

"Yes, sir." He knew it was useless to argue that "the journey" consisted of at most eight miles—that with two strong sons, and at least as many grooms, Caswell hardly needed aid. Useless as well to suggest that they might more wisely wait a day, until the snow stopped or cleared in the warmth of sunlight. Ultimately useless to question any command of his father's, given in just that tone of voice. David was to serve at the Caswells' behest. His own folly had guaranteed it.

He sought out his bleary-eyed batman, Barton, with the

news that he would be traveling that day, then chose to await both his greatcoat and his summons in the library.

Of all that he loved about Braughton, and he loved Braughton very much, the library was perhaps his favorite room, cool on the hottest days, warm now as a fire blazed cheerfully away and the snow still fell. The room's many tall windows always provided ample illumination. Braughton's library, unlike so many in country holdings, was not heavy-paneled and musty. Despite the walls of stone and glass, the room was open, light, and welcoming. As boys he and Myles had explored endlessly among the shelves and ladders. They had known the collection more intimately than had the several tutors Braughton employed. But after so many years away, David felt a stranger.

While he waited, he set it as his task to reacquaint himself with the library's treasures. He was not in the habit of dwelling overmuch on what he could not change. He was, however, well-used to prolonged periods of enforced patience—and of the need to make himself comfortable. Before long he was pleasurably immersed in his chosen volume.

More than an hour passed before he was called to attend the Caswells. After Barton helped him into his greatcoat, David presented himself as escort to his neighbors. Sir Moreton properly introduced the other three members of his family— the two sons and the daughter. As the girl curtsied before him, David caught one glimpse of her face beneath her bonnet, a glimpse abbreviated enough that he was reminded of how much he disliked bonnets.

Since his horse, Incendio, stood tethered to the back of the coach, David knew he would be traveling inside with the family. And just as he'd anticipated, there were at least two grooms with the coachman, making the Caswells' party a veritable army, all to travel such a trifling distance.

He was permitted to face forward, but he soon learned that the arrangement was not intended as a favor. The position deprived him of the pleasure of gazing upon Miss Caswell, who also faced forward from her place at her father's far side. The two brothers sat opposite. David had the dubious reward of confronting sour Morty. The younger brother, Edward Caswell, though still a student at university and trying enough to one's patience, would have been his preference.

Apparently the girl was to be shielded, or neatly confined, as though she were as much an offender as David. He, who had failed to observe propriety, was to be bullied, which struck him as lacking propriety in itself. The ritual seemed so pointless. He wondered what else Sir Moreton could possibly have wanted from him. Though not usually a stickler concerning the niceties, David did puzzle over the Caswells' high-and-mighty sense of entitlement. *He,* after all, was the duke's son, though to his thinking he rarely acted the part. At the moment he sorely wanted to.

For the nonce he was clearly to be kept in suspense and denied any immediate response to his very timely, proper offer.

"You have urgent business today, Sir Moreton?" he asked politely before the horses were set to. "I should have thought it more comfortable for you to outwait the snowstorm's end here at Braughton."

"M' wife is an invalid, my lord," he responded gruffly. "I am rarely away, and then only for short periods. Last night no member of the family was home with her. I do not like to leave her alone."

"I am sorry to hear that, sir." David tried to peer around Caswell to his daughter but succeeded only in catching sight of her gloved hands upon her lap. He wondered how long the mother had been ill. He nearly asked about the prospects for Lady Caswell's recovery but decided the matter was best let lie. Meanwhile, Miss Caswell's slim fingers seemed to taunt him.

"How many sons have you, Sir Moreton?"

"What? Oh—four. Morty here, the eldest. Aged twenty-seven,

is it, Morty? Yes. Then Jack—that is, John Henry. He was a captain in the Light Dragoons."

"Ah! I understood he'd been with the Royal Horse Guards."

"No, no, the Eleventh Light Dragoons. Brought home—oh, two years ago now. And he sold out last summer. Just recently wed, my boy Jack. Livin' in Staffordshire. Then my youngest, Edward, you see opposite. He's up at Cambridge, as you know, and will go to the Bar. And there is Christopher, who is three years older than Billie—er, my daughter, Wilhelmina."

"And is Christopher also at home?"

There was an uneasy silence. Perhaps Christopher was not to be discussed. Something jogged David's memory—some recollection of the ever-present band of boys and urgent yells for "Kit."

Sir Moreton cleared his throat. "When will you be selling out, my lord?" he asked.

"I have not yet decided to do so, sir." David heard the girl's sharp little breath and felt Caswell stiffen beside him. "There has been some suggestion that I might join His Grace the Duke of Wellington in Vienna this spring." He tossed out the possibility as more of a challenge to Caswell than an option for himself. Chas had recommended a stay in Vienna, but David was hungry for home.

"But your regiment—was it sent to America?" Caswell asked.

"Not my regiment of the Guards, sir. I have been serving on the duke's staff, detached from them in any event. But many of the men with whom I served in Spain, some of our very best troops, are now in America, in the Louisiana Territory. With last month's peace, I anticipate their return shortly."

"Kit is wild that he shall have missed everything," Edward volunteered, only to firm his lips at a look from his father.

"He should instead consider himself a lucky man," David observed.

"Denied the many *privations* that have brought you honor and renown?" Morty sneered.

David fixed him with a steady look. "Denied death, perhaps, Mr. Caswell. Assuredly the ultimate *privation*."

In the silence that befell the occupants of the carriage, David proceeded to pull from his greatcoat the volume he had spirited away from the library. The road here outside Braughton was clear but slow; the faint daylight reflecting off the snow gave him enough light to read. Though he considered himself a cordial enough conversationalist in the usual way, the Caswell clan confounded him. He was not often so sharp; his brother, Myles, more frequently employed quick retorts. Yet somehow Myles managed these encounters with finesse. Had Myles said something similar, the Caswells probably would have laughed.

David knew he had always been too frank. But he had made it a rule to keep friends—and to choose not to make enemies. He and Morty Caswell clearly had a difference of outlook.

"What do you have there, my lord?" Edward Caswell asked with some sincerity. David decided that perhaps not all of them were entirely boorish.

"Thucydides, Mr. Edward."

"I have been reading some of the same."

"I must rely on you to explain it to me, then, as I find it heavy going."

Edward Caswell blushed. "I would not presume, my lord . . ."

"I hope I might depend upon you, Mr. Edward," David said gallantly. "My reading has never been of a disciplined nature, though I am extremely fond of books. They are invariably a luxury for soldiers, as your brother, Captain Jack, no doubt knows."

"Surprising to hear there is any luxury denied a Trent," Morty commented.

Again Sir Moreton cleared his throat. "Jack isn't bookish," he said. "Edward and Billie, now—that is, Wilhelmina . . ." He stopped, which was for the best, since David found it irritating that the girl should be discussed as though she were absent. He noted her hands clasped tightly in her lap.

"I heard you were sent down from Oxford," Morty supplied.

"Yes. With but a month to go." David smiled broadly, though in his estimation Mr. Morty deserved a hearty smack. "My dearest wish was to be a scholar."

"You?" Morty snorted rudely. "Hard to believe, given that you were sent down."

David shrugged. "I still had the desire. Is there any higher qualification for scholarship than a love of learning?"

"Surely as Braughton's—as a duke's son—you might have been reinstated?"

"Perhaps. But at the time it did not strike me as quite fair that I should be reinstated when others had no chance for the same." As he smiled, he could feel Billie Caswell's attention. Did she think he made excuses? The incident had certainly influenced his choices since; he had had time and reflection enough to review it.

The carriage came upon a drift of snow blocking the road. The grooms scurried down and cleared a path. During the process David itched to exit the carriage himself. He was used to *doing,* and Thucydides could scarcely distract him from the chill among the company. His father's notion of punishment, in detailing him to escort the Caswells, was proving to be penance indeed.

At the next obstacle of a drift, which looked larger, David opened the door on his side and quickly swung down into the roadway.

"My lord—" Sir Moreton objected, but David had already walked ahead to confer with the grooms and coachman; he held and spoke to the horses—a fine team of matched bays— while the men cleared the wheel tracks. Then, on resuming, he lent a shoulder to pushing the carriage beyond the slick patch of roadway.

When he climbed back into the carriage, he briefly met Billie Caswell's gaze before taking his seat. That one quick look was enough to assure him that what he had imagined of her perfections the previous evening had been no trick of high spirits or candlelight. Her eyes, long-lashed and immense, were only slightly darker than her hair; he could not rid his mind of images of toffee, creamed coffee, amber honey. For David, who now found himself endlessly hungry, Miss Wilhelmina Caswell looked appealingly edible.

There was no hint of the romp about her, but of course that was what she had to be. She had been a terror of a tomboy, a most convincing little hellion; she must still be more than a measure of trouble, else her father would not be attempting to marry her off in such an unfeeling manner. The girl should otherwise have had a proper London season, with better prospects than David Trent.

At the next barrier to movement on the road, Sir Moreton again protested, but given the persistent "milording," David concluded that the gentleman felt obliged to defer to him, at least on minor matters. The day was not so very cold; the snow had at least temporarily stopped. Helping the men gave him an occupation. This time, as he stepped out into the weather, both Morty and Edward stood to join him.

David wondered if they feared he might bolt. With some amusement he made a point of checking on the well-being of his horse tethered behind. He noticed that his man Barton, used to the trials of campaigning, had packed him a saddlebag of necessities; in a pinch David supposed he might escape south to the Channel, and thence to the Continent. He patted Incendio's glossy black neck, murmured encouragement, then moved around to the opposite side of the carriage. When the coachman called "clear," he smoothly stepped in to claim the seat across from Billie Caswell.

He was making a game of holding her gaze; Billie was aware of his design even as she met his challenge. She would not let him believe her ashamed or cowed. *She* had done nothing wrong, though her father might treat her as though she had. And she had always loved to look at David Trent.

He had a wonderful face, older now than she remembered but stronger—certainly less boyish. His dark hair still waved above a high forehead, the blue Trent eyes were striking under dark brows, the suggestion of a smile lingered, lending warmth to his lips and his gaze. In his splendid regimentals the previous night, the breadth of his shoulders had been noticeable; she had quickly forgotten the memory of him as much slighter at twenty-two—Kit's age. In his greatcoat now he seemed to loom, to take up half the carriage, though her father and brothers were not small men. And he sat back against the squabs before her with an ease and an expression that was confidence itself.

She had adored him for as long as she could remember.

Her gloved hands formed fists as she at last looked away, out the window to the side. She made the mistake of firming her lips, only to desist immediately. She could feel the intensity of his concentration on her face. The sensation was not unpleasant—he had watched her closely last night as well—but she colored. She wished she had more control. She wished—oh, she wished that they had met again under different circumstances, that they had not been seen and trapped. That he had not been forced to offer—and forced to resent her.

Father could not understand why she was refusing to consider Lord David's proposal. She had always declared it the dearest wish of her heart. Indeed, every member of her family knew of her years-long infatuation with Braughton's younger son. They had asked her what more she could possibly desire.

The answer to that, though unvoiced, had been "reciprocity"—some correspondence of feeling. *That he should care as much as I do.* Or at least as much as she had always believed she had. She did not want David Trent as a sacrifice. But how else were they to satisfy the Caswell honor?

Her gaze returned to him, to find that his own attention had not wavered. She knew with certainty that he had never once dreamed of *her*. He had not even realized she was a girl.

"Morty," she said into the silence, even as she stared into what she considered "the blue" of that gaze. Morty now sat where David had, at her father's other side. "You must pass the major his Thucydides."

She continued to meet his gaze as the book was dutifully passed across to Edward and on to the seat at Major Trent's side.

"I have a much preferred pastime at the moment, Miss Caswell," he said. For a second he let his gaze fall again to her lips, long enough that she felt a blush seek her cheeks. She pointedly turned her attention out the window.

When the carriage abruptly halted once more, Billie anticipated his exit. But this time, as Edward and Morty sprang to action, David Trent stubbornly kept his seat. He actually had the gall to smile at her.

"Are you planning a season in town this spring, Miss Caswell?" he asked.

"Most certainly *you* will have a say in *that,* my lord," her father said quickly, leaning toward him with urgency.

"And how so, sir? How can it affect me?"

"What! Do you want the girl or not?"

Billie drew a sharp breath, waiting for David's definitive "no."

His eyebrows shot high. "Surely Miss Caswell must determine what *she* wants, sir?"

The question was much to the point; he had masterfully called her father's bluff in asking. Sir Moreton responded with silence. Billie had an insight as to just how keen and purposeful an officer David Trent must be, the more so when his gaze settled on her with a marked decrease in warmth. He must have deduced, correctly, that *she* was the obstacle to clarity in this matter—that *she* was the one delaying an answer, weighing his offer in the balance, holding his feet to the fire. She was determined to speak with him first.

He tried another tack. Once her brothers returned to their seats and the carriage was again rolling, Lord David let one of his boots rest casually against her skirts. Billie glared at him and attempted to shift her position, but she was squeezed to the side of the bench by her father and Morty, and the major's legs were indisputably long.

She wanted to ignore so slight a contact, to act as though it were accidental, but by avoiding his gaze she knew she acknowledged it. She focused on the scenery outside. The snow had resumed. They had already spent almost two hours traveling a distance that usually required less than one; her impatience for the trip to end found relief in occasional soundless sighs.

When the major's other knee touched her skirt, she glanced at him, prepared to utter a rebuke. But he was now slouched against the seat back, his arms crossed over his chest and his eyes closed in sleep. Next to her, her father had succumbed to the same state of oblivion. That the men could doze in such uncomfortable circumstances amazed her.

Edward was peacefully reading Lord David's Greek text.

Billie studied David's features. Last night he had reminded her too starkly of her foolishness as a youngster. At age twelve, intending to shoot him with "Cupid's dart," she had most accurately sent an arrow flying from ambush—straight to David Trent's shoulder. She vividly recalled Kit's triumphant yell, how David had reeled and tumbled from his horse, her own stunned horror at his too-real pallor. They had knelt by his side and watched numbly as the blood pooled upon his shirt. He had hissed to them to fetch Rawlinson, the old stable

master, and Kit had scrambled up upon David's horse and ridden away like the very devil. But Billie had been left to face
David's accusing stare.

"You . . . did this?" he had asked. And then he'd sworn at
her, repeatedly and incomprehensibly in French, before his
swoon had spared her.

Within minutes help had arrived from Braughton. She and
Kit had been sent home, to wait in fear of a reckoning that
never arrived. Word had reached them that Lord David survived the ordeal. Billie had trusted and prayed that he would,
but she'd had no opportunity to apologize. In the subsequent
year she had seen him only twice more, and then only from a
distance. He had left for war on the Peninsula without a word
from her.

Last night he'd claimed the shoulder still pained him in the
cold. She wondered if it troubled him now in the snow. The
wound must have inconvenienced him all the long years at
war. And as her pensive gaze left his shoulder and rose again
to his face, she caught the steady scrutiny in his.

He was not asleep, if he had ever been, and both his boots
now neatly bracketed her cloaked skirts in a manner that was
simply not acceptable.

Billie managed to turn one of her ankles and bring the pressure of her instep down atop his toes. With his grimace she
had to believe that, had he thought to play with her or to play
upon her guilty sympathies, he must now consider himself
corrected.

"At last," Morty muttered as they entered the drive to the
manor. "We might almost have walked it in this time."

"Some of us might have been limping by now though, Mr.
Caswell." His gaze on hers, David sat up farther, carefully removing his boots from her reach.

Billie could not stop her smile. She looked out the window.
She dared not glance at him again, for fear she might laugh
outright.

When they drew up to the house, Morty moved to unlatch the door facing the front and the waiting footman. But the major swiftly opened the door opposite and, leaping out *sans* the step, pulled Billie out the far side. Before her startled senses could recover, he had pressed his lips to hers. With equal speed he put her away from him.

He easily parried her raised, open palm. "We are betrothed," he told her smoothly.

"You are mistaken!"

"Then you must say so, Billie Caswell."

She swallowed and raised her chin. She could hear her father and brothers mounting the steps to the house.

"What happened to *'querida'*?" she challenged.

He brought his face very close to hers once more. " '*Querida*' is still there, if you wish it. But take care how you punish a man, Miss Caswell. It must be proportionate to the offense."

He stepped away from her to the back of the carriage and moved to free his horse.

"What are you about there, Lord David?" her father called from above. "You must come along inside here for some dinner."

"I think I'd best be getting back, Sir Moreton, before the weather grows much worse."

"Enjoy a meal, my lord, and let your horse be cared for. The snow is nothing to speak of."

Billie thought her father had not sounded half so pleasant all day; at home he was making an effort at courtesy. Yet she wished they need no longer play at propriety. That David Trent should think she *punished* him was galling. Surely having been forced to offer at all had been the punishment.

She had walked on up to her father's side. *Let him go,* she silently urged him. *Please, just let him go.* Her gaze as cold as she could muster, she willed the major to be on his way. They

might talk another time. But the perverse man seemed to delight in crossing her.

"Well, then," he said, his smile provoking. "Perhaps for an
hour or two, sir. And we might finish discussing our business."

Chapter Three

They stomped into the hall. Billie was relieved to find it presentable this evening, not—as seemed too frequent of late—redolent of damp or of Morty's hounds or stale tobacco. Still, she remained uneasy, for the major's last comment had sounded like a threat. She thought he must mean to move forward with an engagement, as mad as such a course might be.

At least her father had no desire to leap abruptly into discussion of dowries.

"You'll excuse me, my lord," he said gruffly, as Tate came forward to take their coats. "My wife will be most anxious to see me."

"Certainly, sir." As Lord David was relieved of his greatcoat, he subjected the hall to such close regard that Billie chose to feel defensive. Her father made his way upstairs, leaving the major to Billie and her brothers.

"How long has Lady Caswell been ill?" he asked.

"Forever," Edward mumbled, shrugging out of his own coat. "Or seems like."

"You might recall it, Trent," Morty said sharply, "as the last visit she made was to Braughton eight years ago."

"I regret I do not remember, Mr. Caswell. Do you blame that visit for her subsequent indisposition?"

Morty flushed to his ears. "Not at all. Just meant—that was the last time she went calling, is all."

"I am sorry to hear it. She does not improve?"

"She has her good days—and many more bad," Edward said glumly. "If you'll pardon me, Major, I have some translations. . . ." And he departed, followed precipitously by Morty, who mumbled about seeing to necessary correspondence before dinner. Morty seemed eager to avoid the overwhelming responsibility of acting as host in his own home. Or else he had properly gauged that David Trent too frequently outwitted him.

The major smiled at Billie just as she felt most acutely her family's rude desertion.

"You must pardon them, my lord. They are not . . ." she attempted. "They are not usually so thoughtless."

"We are all at ease in our own homes, Miss Caswell," he offered smoothly, making a shallow bow, "and it has been a tiring day. I know 'tis merely an oversight that we should have been left alone."

"They trust me," she countered. "Would you imply they should not trust you?"

"We shall see."

His small smile disconcerted her. She turned to Tate and asked him to have a maid start the fire in the drawing room. She felt the major's gaze as she made the request. Her effort to supplement their company must have been all too obvious.

"You study my home, Major," she said, lifting her chin a fraction as she showed him into the drawing room. "You find fault with it?"

"On the contrary, Miss Caswell. All is order and comfort. The opposite of what I should have expected of a household of men—men left so long in want of Lady Caswell's influence. I credit you, young as you are, with meeting the challenge."

She felt the color in her cheeks and turned away. "Dinner will be at least an hour, Major. Would you care for some refreshment beforehand?"

"Coffee would be welcome, thank you." As Billie arranged for a tray, the major wandered to the piano and idly pressed several keys. "Do you play, Miss Caswell, or was this your mother's instrument?"

"Both," she said. " 'Tis still my mother's, and I play it. Mama insisted that I claim at least one of a lady's accomplishments."

"She must be pleased then—that you claim many."

To contain another blush, she stared him straight in the eyes. "No doubt you practiced such flummery in Paris, my lord."

"I had little time in Paris to practice much of anything, Miss Caswell. Lately I've spent too much time traveling, including three trips between Paris and Vienna in as many months. The winter has been a harsh one. 'Twas not the holiday you envisage." Again he pressed his fingers to the keys. "Will you play something?"

"I am not very good."

"I should imagine you are exceptionally good."

The compliment disconcerted her. However lightly proffered, it was welcome and somehow restorative. Her family was prone to tease rather than to commend; even their urging her at this man, even their insistence on a betrothal, was an extension of all the teasing. After all, such a tie was what she had always claimed to want, for as long as she had known of David Trent.

"Perhaps later," she said, looking away from him.

"Then, as we've been granted this bit of privacy, you might instead answer two questions for me." When her attention returned to him, he asked bluntly, "Why should you continue with this? And why should you resist a season?"

"I do not resist a season! In fact, our plans for a visit to town are well along. My father only meant, in the carriage, that now *you* might have some say in whether we go or not."

"One assumes that if you were welcoming a season, you are not averse to marriage?"

"Of course I am not 'averse to marriage'! I object only to compelling you—"

"And so I ask my first question for a second time—why should you allow me so much of a claim? Last night we did nothing so irredeemable, certainly nothing to warrant such an extreme response. My offer was proper but not entirely necessary. Our fathers know as much. They are not so Gothic in their notions as to press *you,* however much they feel *I* might owe. If *you* did not want this to go forward, it would not."

"But they know you kissed me. . . ."

"Hardly."

"Hardly?"

" 'Twas a mere suggestion. You found that slight attempt sufficient?"

"Sufficient?"

He smiled at her, though his gaze remained watchful.

"Major Trent," she continued coldly, "I will leave you to your coffee."

She turned to go, but at his low and serious, "Billie," she turned.

"Do not leave," he went on. "Forgive me. I forget you are still very young."

"I shall be nineteen in March."

"As I said." He smiled. "Now do stay. Because I think you must explain yourself. We will not have many opportunities—"

"I must explain, but you needn't?"

"Oh, I am easily understood." Again that smile held her. "I danced with a beautiful stranger on New Year's Eve and yielded to overwhelming impulse. Though the yielding may have been unwise, there is little incomprehensible in it. I wished to kiss you and endeavored to do so. Absent an interruption, I should have been more thorough." He studied her furious complexion. "I cannot plead a lack of interest, though I confess matrimony was far from my mind. For your part—it is not gallant of me to mention, I know—you did accompany me last night." Before she could protest, he added, "Nevertheless, you might now claim almost anything shy of abduction and be believed. Equally, as the injured party, you might snap your fingers and have done with this business. I will do as I must, should you desire it. But do you desire it? I should like to understand. I am too blunt a fellow to play at absurdities."

"You are indeed 'blunt,' Major."

"I am trained to it, Miss Caswell. 'Tis preferable to misunderstandings, or retreat."

"This is not some . . . some battlefield!"

His answering smile mystified her. For some reason his amusement placed her at a disadvantage.

He shrugged. "We must be honest with each other—our futures are at stake. Surely the Billie Caswell who roamed the county with her brothers is capable of candor. Or have years of proper schooling robbed you of it?"

She felt the sting of the question—and the challenge. He had understood that in her—the desire not to forget herself, not to assume airs. She had long derided the artifice and manipulations of her school fellows. Her defiance at once seemed petty, and yet—though he urged her to be candid—she still had to take care. He would never understand how devotedly she had favored him.

She drew breath, prepared to relay something of sense, but a footman entered just then with the tray of coffee. Thankfully, the major waved the man away rather than have a cup poured out for him. Billie was left to meet his inquiring gaze.

"You must understand the . . . the circumstances, Major. My family has known for many years of my . . . *admiration* for you—from the time I was no more than seven or eight." She swallowed as she watched his eyebrows shoot high. "I never spoke of it, but my brothers, quite understandably, became aware of my . . . fascination. I used to follow you about. 'Tis how I knew of the weir. I was there." Her chin rose. "My brothers teased me mercilessly. Of course my parents came to hear of my . . . regard as well. I had thought, with my schooling taking me so much away, that all of them would have for-

gotten. But last night, even before we danced, Morty made
some comment." She gestured dismissively and started to pace.
"I suspect my father must have mentioned my sentiments to
your father at some point, that the two of them should have
proposed anything so serious as an arrangement. Papa told me
last summer that he thought His Grace, your father, had raised
the possibility with you. I did not know whether you had indeed been approached. But 'tis their notion, not mine, my lord."
She straightened her shoulders as she again met his gaze. "It
seems I must pay in full for a childish partiality. Though I am
no longer a child."

She could not see his face. He had turned from her to pour
himself some coffee, though the act was in no way inattentive.
In fact, she was conscious of the alertness in his stance. Even
turned away from her, he listened.

He raised the cup, holding it casually free of its saucer and
about the rim, as one might hold a pewter cup in an alehouse.
His gaze focused somewhere on the carpet. As he took a sip,
she could read little besides consideration in his expression.

"Few of us," he said, at last returning the cup to its saucer,
"are held accountable for youthful . . . preferences in quite the
manner that you have been, Miss Caswell. I thank you for being so forthright. I was unkind to imply you might ever be
otherwise. Still—well, *les premières amours.*" He shrugged.
"Puppy love. My *grand-mère* is a very wise woman."

"Your *grand-mère*? The Dowager Duchess? She knows of
this as well?"

He shook his head. "No. She is only an observer, but a most
astute one. You've nothing to fear from her. In fact, I think I
must have her look to your interests in town."

"That is not necessary, my lord. I would never presume—"

"Where will you stay?"

"At my aunt's—my father's sister's. My aunt Ephie, Miss
Euphemia Caswell, has a house on Grafton Street. And Morty
shall come as well."

"From what I've seen, he will make a most disagreeable escort," he said curtly. "Why does he dislike me so?"

"Morty? Why, you must not remember. But he, living here, has had little opportunity to forget. He once held the squire's daughter, Cora Peebles, in some esteem. Yes, I see that you recall her. I think Morty even thought to offer for Cora some six years ago. Before you left for the Peninsula. But at the Braughton assembly that spring, you stood up with Cora twice. And after your attentions and your patronage, she had no time for Morty."

"Cora Peebles! I can hardly picture the girl. Though I remember dancing many hours that night. I set off for Portugal within the week. I assure you, Miss Caswell, I cannot be charged with an indiscretion at *that* event."

"Oh, I know it—Morty knows it. Even Cora must admit it. But she was quite above herself and would have naught else to do with Morty. You forget that everything of Braughton, of doings at the hall or in town, is of greatest import. When we are away, it is not so very momentous. That is, it never seems of much account. But I have just revealed my own folly. I cannot criticize Cora's."

"You were a child." At her silence, he moved closer. "But we come back 'round to our difficulty. And I must ask you again—what do you want?"

For a few seconds she could only stare at him, at the warm blue gaze that never failed to hold her. Despite all to which she might confess, as juvenile and irrational as the confession might be, she still wanted *him*. But that could not be acknowledged. She could scarcely admit it to herself.

"To speak frankly, Major . . ."

"Yes?"

"I would not refuse to marry you. But I object to *your* objection."

"I do not object. I am here."

She thought he smiled too easily.

"You are most polite. But you know you have been forced."

"Forced or not, Miss Caswell, I do not object." He considered her. "Do you seek to induce me to cry off, to flee the country or behave in some other shameful manner? What is the point of your season, after all, if not to catch a husband?"

"I don't plan to 'catch a husband'!"

"You would simply prefer another."

"*You* are not inclined."

"I could be."

"I shouldn't wish you to labor at it," she said sharply.

"Perhaps I ought to kiss you once more."

"That is not the solution to anything."

"No?"

She looked down. She had never noticed before that the carpet held a small lotus design. She drew a deep breath. "I think I should like more time," she said. " 'Twould pacify my father."

"Well, that is easily managed. How much time would you wish? The season? A year?"

"Oh, no—not nearly so much! A month might do, so that I—so that I might appear to develop another . . ."

"Distraction?"

Again her face warmed. "Another interest, certainly. Which should not be unusual, in anticipation of our departure for town. My interest needn't be more involved than an eagerness to freely attend the events of the season, such as parties and dances. I might be expected to have second thoughts, to be excited on the eve of a visit and to wish to . . . explore some choices. That at least must be understandable." She thought he watched her with a particular care.

"Then a month it is, Miss Caswell. How we proceed at the end of it is, of course, entirely your decision. I am in no hurry."

Billie's chin rose. "Nor am I. I merely please my father—as you please yours."

"Oh, I think I might be relied upon to please myself as well."

He did not quite smile as he studied her face. "You know I am too old for you," he added, as though he seriously contemplated a match—so much so that she swallowed.

"If you persist on that topic, my lord, I shall think you most limited in conversation." At his quick smile she added lightly, "You are scarcely ten years older than I. You are not yet twenty-nine."

"I suspect you even know my birth date." He tilted his head as he eyed her. "I caution you, Miss Caswell. Whatever you believe you know of me is not enough. You may have observed me as a youth, but I have been away a very long time."

"People do not change. Not in their essentials."

"Don't they? Is that for good or ill?" When she did not respond to his smile, he said, "I must suppose, then, that though you are now a young lady of fashion, at heart you are still a hoyden. One who would see me carried wounded off the field?"

"I did not mean to harm you."

His hand rose to his left shoulder. "I should certainly hate to see you angered!"

She would not tell him the truth of that encounter. Her candor extended only so far. She struggled to think of the present.

"Would you say, then, that we—that we understand each other, my lord?"

"As well as man and woman might." Again he drew her attention. Again he was smiling. She had always thought him good-humored but did not like to imagine he exercised his high spirits at her expense. At once she feared that even the most temporary of arrangements might prove too dangerous to her heart.

"Would it not be more sensible," she offered abruptly, "for me to release you from any obligation now? Tonight?"

"You said you wanted time."

"But if that is not the wisest course . . ."

"You convince me that it *is* the wisest course. Your first instincts are sound. We mustn't be hasty. We must maneuver within the small space allowed us. Else our well-meaning parents will feel frustrated in their aims. As you say, this is a union they desire. They mustn't consider themselves aggrieved or crossed in any way. Anything that might further *their* friendship and comity is for the best. We might even find it apropos to extend your required month, Miss Caswell. By the time you reach town—when? March?" At her nod, he continued. "By March you might boast of having rejected one offer—mine, that is. I understand such a romantic history heightens the interest of others."

"You would make this a game?"

"It is a game, my dear. Though its aim is anything but frivolous. 'Tis best you realize it. Consider that I prepare you for the game's intricacies. I would suggest, to your own advantage, that you play me upon your line. Only as your patience allows, of course."

"I wouldn't wish to appear fickle."

He smiled. "Certainly not."

Her glance at him was impatient. "You are remarkably generous with your time, Major—and with your reputation."

"I am on leave," he said mildly. "And my pride is of a different variety. 'Twould probably be of benefit to me to be perceived as a spurned suitor. I might even find a generous heart to take pity on me."

Again she looked to the floor. "Do you seek a generous heart?"

"Oh, always."

When she looked up, he was considering her.

"We appear to have settled our affairs, then, Miss Caswell, and since it is, after all, the New Year, won't you now entertain me with a tune?"

As she thought further conversation more than likely to betray her abiding affection, she went dutifully to the piano and took a seat. Her fingers were not quite steady, but they warmed as she ran them over the keys. She chose a simple, ancient tune, "The Soldier's Delight." As she played, he came to stand by the piano. The drawing room, in reality so large, at once seemed stiflingly close.

"Will you join me, Major?" she asked. "By singing?" She knew she made an effort at composure.

He shook his head. "I will not spoil your rendition."

"You shouldn't demur. I know you have a fine tenor."

"Too many in this county seem to remark it. One would think I had been endlessly bellowing about the countryside. I must have worn out my welcome long ago." He viewed the music from over her shoulder. " 'The Soldier's Delight.' Do you know what that is, Miss Caswell?"

"Why, I should suppose—the call to battle. The honor and glory of war."

Again he shook his head. "Any soldier's delight is home. A safe return home."

For a second her fingers faltered. But as she continued to play, he did join her, by lightly humming the tune. She thought *her* delight must surely be hearing that deeply masculine accompaniment and having him stand so near.

At a loud disturbance in the hall, she stopped abruptly. The front door banged back upon its hinges as a cold blast of air found its way even to the warmth of the fireside. Tate's soft protest rose above the tramp of boots upon the hall's tiled floor.

"S'blight—Trent's s'blight—cursed neighbors!" The slurred, accusing words came from the door, where Tate and the portly Braughton innkeeper, Mr. Puddiway, attempted to prop her slumping brother Christopher between them.

"Kit!" She was instantly upon her feet. Lord David stepped back as she slipped around the piano and hurried across the room.

David's first thought was that the boy might have been Billie's twin—the newcomer was so clearly her brother, with the same striking coloring and fine features. A second glance confirmed that this was no boy but a youth of at least twenty-two or three, and already showing the signs of dissipation that would soon make him look older yet. His collar hung limply. He needed a shave and almost everything else. Were it not for the good offices of Tate and Puddiway, Kit Caswell would have been a heap upon the floor.

David stepped forward to relieve the two older men of their burden.

"Allow me," he said, taking the lad's full weight upon his own left side. Kit Caswell seemed to make some small effort at rebellion but then collapsed even more heavily against him.

"I thank'ee, milord," Puddiway gasped. "Had a sight o' trouble gittin' 'im out from town, what with the snow startin' agin. But I knew Miss Caswell would be worryin', so's I brought him meself. Though we're plump full with New Year's guests and the missus readyin' supper . . ."

David managed to slip his free hand inside his tunic, where he retrieved a sovereign.

"Appreciate it, Puddy," he said, handing the coin to him. "You'll want to be heading back to your hearth."

"Oh, yessir, milord, uh—Major. Thankee. Best o' the New Year to ye, milord."

" 'Thankee,' " Kit Caswell mimicked sullenly, as Puddiway departed. "Milord—nothing!"

"Kit!" Billie was pulling at her brother's sleeve, as though so slight an effort might aid in keeping him conscious, or courteous. The mixed anxiety and affection in her voice made David's lips firm.

"Where should you like him, Miss Caswell?" he managed impatiently. Though thin, the youth was difficult to hold upright. David expected him to pass out or be thoroughly sick at any moment.

"Oh, upstairs, please, Major—if you can?"

He nodded and hoisted the baggage up farther upon one shoulder. As he carried his load up the stairs, with the elderly butler providing an occasional steadying hand, Sir Moreton came out upon an upper landing.

"Kit!" he exclaimed, in such a tone that David decided the name must often be spoken with exasperation. "Where have you been?"

"Mr. Puddiway just brought him from the inn, Father," Billie said, as Sir Moreton moved to aid them in maneuvering Kit through a narrow bedroom door.

David slid his burden onto the bed and stepped back to let the others stretch the wastrel out upon the duvet. He found he could not quite appreciate the solicitude with which Billie eased a blanket across her brother. David viewed the disheveled lump upon the bed with scarcely concealed distaste.

"Has he been ill?" he asked, noting Kit Caswell's pallor and the beads of sweat upon his brow.

"He has not been well for some time, my lord," Sir Moreton answered gruffly, drawing him hastily from the room. "Come, Billie. Tate, do send my own man to see to him. Lord David, you must be eager for your dinner."

"Not at all, sir. In fact, I believe I mustn't stay." He heard Billie Caswell's swiftly drawn breath as they made their way back downstairs. "Puddiway said the snow has started once more. But if you please—I should like a brief word."

Sir Moreton nodded and led the way to his study off the back of the hall. David could feel Billie's gaze upon him as he followed her father. He wondered if she could read his thought, which was at that moment intensely clear to him: she ought to welcome an establishment of her own. She could never have deserved being saddled with such a churlish lot of relatives.

He knew that view influenced his manner—that he was more peremptory and unyielding with the Caswell patriarch than he'd intended to be. But, given his desire to depart and

Caswell's obvious distraction, a brief interview served. David repeated his offer for the daughter, relayed her request for time, and promised his own attentions as long as she desired them. He stressed that no date had been set for a wedding and that no effort should be initiated to draw up settlements, because the lady had not yet ascertained her wishes. Miss Caswell still anticipated her season.

Sir Moreton appeared to find the interchange satisfactory, at least to the extent of warmly shaking hands with him. When they parted in the hall, Caswell again excused himself to return upstairs. And David asked that his horse be brought around.

"You are certain you must leave now, Major?" Billie asked from the drawing-room door.

"I fear I must, Miss Caswell," he said, shrugging into his greatcoat. "I would not tax you with a guest on such an evening."

" 'Tis no burden," she assured him, though her smile was slight.

No burden certainly, he thought, *compared to that of your family.*

As she stood there so obviously proud and alone, her beauty struck him as something extraordinary. Whatever elegance had been borne through the Caswell line had distilled itself in her. And that sudden recognition struck him strangely silent.

"It is much too cold to ride back tonight, my lord," she added.

" 'Tis not cold at all. The snow assures it. I have confronted much worse, Miss Caswell."

"What did you say to Papa—to my father—just now?"

"That I am at your command." He bowed. "And only your command, for as long as you wish it. You understand me?"

She was studying his face. "You said earlier that I 'punish' you."

He smiled. She was young indeed to have found any hurt in

that. "You misunderstood. The punishment was not the necessity to offer, or being held to an offer. I brought that on myself, after all. I referred only to your lack of clarity. But now we are in accord, are we not?"

She nodded and moved with him to the door.

"All is well, then, Miss Caswell. You have your time. I'd suggest you not waste it in babying your brother."

" 'Babying'?" Her instant temper surprised him. "I suppose you are so used to the privileges of Braughton that you cannot imagine . . . that you . . . Oh! You forget yourself, Major!"

"What the devil!" In confronting her wildly pink cheeks, his answering, astonishing pique required unexpected control. "Has the whiner infected you with excuses and resentments? *That* would be poor recompense for all your affection and care. But 'tis the way of such spoiled youngsters. I have seen too much of it, Miss Caswell. And I fear I must correct you. My brother and I have had privileges enough, as you rightly point out, but we have never been indulged."

"You are too proud, my lord," she said. "Surely it is not *your* place to determine whether you have been indulged. And that you should dare attack my family! Whatever we have— whatever you believe you arranged here this evening—is at an end. I release you from any understanding. Now—this minute! We have no agreement. You need not contact me, or my father, ever again!"

" 'Attack' your family? You mistake me, Miss Caswell. And you take this too much to heart. Say what you will, *I* refuse to let the blighter interfere with us in the slightest. Does he demand so much, or do you volunteer it?"

"Good-bye, Major." As she wheeled from him, he caught her elbow.

"No, Billie—*querida*—" He leaned to kiss her, but catching the look in her amber eyes, he lightly tapped her chin instead. "You almost make me wish that the year might continue as it began. A kiss is sorely tempting. But 'twould only confuse you further." He restrained a smile. "I shall be patient. You shall see me again soon, sweet, as promised—within the month." And with that pledge, and now feeling quite warm enough for a much longer journey, he turned out into the snow.

Chapter Four

Billie did not see him again within the month, or even within two. The New Year was only ten days old when word reached them of the disastrous battle at New Orleans, where more than two thousand British troops, many of them seasoned veterans of long years in the Peninsular campaign, had been felled by a relative handful of Americans. And the shocking defeat had occurred, perhaps most tragically, just as Britain had at last believed itself at peace. News of December's peace agreements, celebrated by the European allies over the holidays, simply had not traveled across the Atlantic in time to prevent the continuation of hostilities and the carnage on American soil.

Even the Duke of Wellington's brother-in-law, Major-General Sir Edward Pakenham, had been lost at New Orleans.

Lord David's regiment of House Guards, the Coldstream regiment, had not been in America or Louisiana, but as he'd previously served with many of the other officers on the Peninsula, he must have felt the loss keenly. With receipt of the news, he apparently had not waited to be summoned. He had left Leicestershire immediately to return to Paris and Wellington.

Before leaving, he had troubled to convey his apologies to Miss Caswell; he regretted the delay in settling their affairs. In a most economical three lines he had recommended that she not allow uncertainty regarding their status to influence her in the slightest. He assured her that he was, as he had always been, hers alone. She must do, as he termed it, as she "thought best."

She knew she would have married him the next day—had he loved her. But he'd admitted only attraction, an attraction that pressure to wed could scarcely further. She had promptly told her father that Lord David would not suit after all.

Sir Moreton had merely harrumphed, claiming that it was "early days yet" and infuriatingly advising her that she did not know her own mind. He had refused to relay her withdrawal to David's father, the Duke of Braughton. Given her father's willfulness and David's absence, Billie resigned herself to remaining to all outward appearances attached, though there was nothing to it at all. And that situation would continue as long as she and Lord David were parted.

By the last week in February she had moved on to town, to her aunt Euphemia's and the start of the social season.

Aunt Ephie had claimed, too enthusiastically in Billie's view, that her niece's tenuous betrothal was enviable—that any other young woman making her debut would leap at the possibility of marrying "into" Braughton. Despite Billie's explanation, despite her protests, Ephie assured her that there need be no substance to the perception, that it was not necessary that a marriage ever take place—that to society expectation was all. In that Ephie echoed what David had suggested at the New Year. But Billie could not be as sanguine. She did not consider her situation enviable; she found it disturbingly deceitful. Though everyone else, including her family, might perceive her as promised, she knew she had released David Trent from obligation almost as soon as he had undertaken it. She had been most emphatic on the doorstep at New Year's. Though she now regretted her temper, and though her sentiments warred with her sense, she would not compel him to wed. She was determined on it.

But she did not know how she was to act. The other young

ladies in town had accepted her presence within their circle as posing little threat, serving rather to attract male attention that could not be fixed upon her, as she was already engaged. Billie sought pleasure in the season's entertainments, but she knew her behavior must always be irreproachable—befitting a Braughton bride, though that was not what she was to be, and though the lucky gentleman was nowhere to be seen.

She had not slept soundly for weeks, and even Ephie's excellent cook could not tempt her to sample much in the way of meals. On any given day Billie wondered just where Major Trent might be.

Her growing abstraction interfered with the simplest decisions.

She spent an inordinate amount of time considering her wardrobe for that afternoon's call. The Dowager Duchess of Braughton, Lord David's *grand-mère*, had invited Billie and her aunt to visit. Billie could only assume that the invitation had been sent at David's instigation. She had heard nothing from him and little of him since his departure in January, but that did not mean he had been as silent with his family.

She knew she had no call to feel ill-used; there were, after all, larger matters pending. The Duke of Wellington had moved on from Paris to represent Great Britain at the Congress of Vienna, which august body of allies still worked at hammering out a post-war structure for all the European states. Billie had heard enough conversation to gather that small smattering of politics. She had consulted the atlas almost daily. She had to believe—given issues of such importance—that the intricacies of one trifling, personal alliance could scarcely signify.

She tossed aside an emerald silk sash.

"You do not like that, miss?" Simms, her maid, sounded surprised.

"'Tis well enough. But not just now." Billie had hardly glanced at the thing. "I will not wear a sash."

"But with Her Grace—"

"It is not important, Simms. I assure you, I shall look presentable. As I remember, Her Grace is a woman of considerable good sense."

"Yes, miss," Simms agreed dubiously. Billie guessed that in the young maid's opinion, nothing was too grand for a duchess.

Her aunt Ephie clearly felt the same.

"The gown is most tasteful, Wilhelmina," she observed with a frown, "but shouldn't you prefer something a bit more . . . colorful?"

"I look well enough in this, Auntie. I've no wish to fuss."

"'Tis far from 'fussing' to take some particular care. The Dowager Duchess—"

"Must be nearing eighty, Auntie. And I understand she was recently ill. I observed her at the New Year. Her own style is elegant but understated. I can hardly appall her if I mimic her own taste. And, truth be told, it is my own preference."

Ephie pursed her lips but clearly knew when to desist. Billie had never been one to yield readily to claims of fashion. She had a stubborn sense of what looked suitable and had little patience with unnecessary embellishment.

So her plain white gown with muted cream underskirt and trim would do very well—it heightened the red highlights in her hair and the healthy glow of her complexion. She quickly tamped any curiosity as to whether Lord David would have appreciated the effect and reminded herself that, whatever its prompting, he had most opportunely and precipitously seized upon his freedom, even if he had neglected to acknowledge it publicly.

"I wonder," Ephie mused aloud on their way in the carriage, "if Lord David suggested this invitation."

"He told me at the New Year that he might have his *grandmère* aid me this spring. But, given his hurried departure, I suspect he forgot to propose it." Billie concentrated hard on observing the bustling afternoon activity on the street about them. Many people had been filtering into town from the countryside, intent on protesting the proposed higher prices for grain, an issue to be debated in Parliament. The mood of the crowds of small farmers, laborers, out-of-work tradesmen, and former soldiers grew increasingly threatening. "His father, the duke, probably recommended the invitation," she continued with a frown. " 'Tis our fathers, after all, who forward the match."

"Now, Billie, do not start again! When you speak so, you sound much too bitter for eighteen."

"Nineteen, Auntie. Saturday."

"I know very well when your birthday is, missy. We have that special supper laid in after the Loomises' tea."

"Yes, ma'am. And I am most achingly appreciative of your generosity. But my point was that I am old enough to know my own mind. And I am certainly old enough to understand my circumstances. You mustn't carry on as though—as though this is some grand romance! Or as though we now attend an audience with the Prince Regent."

" 'Tis close," her aunt muttered, before turning to look pointedly out the window.

They completed the rest of the journey in an obstinate absence of conversation. Billie was in no mood to placate her aunt. But as they stepped out at the foot of the duchess' front steps, Billie leaned to kiss Ephie quickly on the cheek.

"Do not fret so," she urged her aunt softly, by way of insuring her own composure as well.

"Ah, Billie!" Ephie said, in a tone that Billie could have interpreted as either fond or exasperated.

The Dowager Duchess of Braughton chose to live almost year-round in town, in the house that had sheltered the Dukes of Braughton for the previous two hundred years. The mansion had been rebuilt twice, and now evidenced all the sturdy elegance of which one of the country's oldest and most illustrious families could boast. From the busts of distinguished ancestors in the hall to the sweeping velvet drapes, oiled wood, and glistening silver in the drawing room, all the appointments were rich and exquisitely understated. And the elderly woman who greeted them from the fireside was, though frail and wrapped in the depths of a wing chair, as splendid as her surroundings.

Billie's quick glance noted the traces of the duchess' youthful looks—the white hair that had once been blond, the high cheekbones, and the clear, sky-blue gaze. An openness, a charm of expression, lingered. As Billie curtsied, she thought again, as she had thought at the New Year, that David's *grand-mère* appeared to shimmer, in some lively, gemlike manner.

"So I have here two Miss Caswells," the duchess exclaimed with her pronounced French accent. Her smile was warm and happy. "May I call you Miss Wilhelmina?"

"You must call me Billie, Your Grace."

"Billie." She pronounced it more precisely and elegantly than it had ever been spoken before. "Yes, it suits you. How charming you look today, my dear."

And Billie thanked her before glancing triumphantly at Ephie.

Refreshments must have been ordered the minute they arrived, because a number of servants, laden with various trays, entered the room as Billie and Ephie took seats near their hostess.

"We might have other callers while you visit with me," the duchess said. "I hope you do not mind. Town becomes occupied, most busy, here in March."

It was, of course, not their place to mind in the least.

"You left Leicestershire when, then, Miss Billie?

"Just one week ago, Your Grace."

"And what have you seen, what have you done, in that week?"

The answer sounded rather exhausting to Billie's own ears as she listed her activities—never had she been so measured and primped and squeezed in her life. But most of the expenditure of energy and money had been directed to what was yet to come.

"You will dance at Almack's?" the duchess asked.

"We await the vouchers, Your Grace," Aunt Ephie said. "Wilhelmina has yet to be presented at court."

"I shall see that you receive your vouchers shortly, Miss Caswell," the duchess said with a wave of her tiny white hand. "Such a system! Absurd!" She looked rather imperious as she dismissed the most selective process in town. "And are any of your brothers here, Billie, to escort you?"

"My oldest brother, Moreton, is here, Your Grace. And my next-to-youngest, Christopher—Kit—is in town, but he spends much of his time at his . . . at his clubs."

"Does he? Ah! The gaming! My own brother was most enamored of it! Phillipe was—I regret that Phillipe was often very bad, though I loved him most dearly. And you have more brothers?"

So Billie told her of Captain Jack, now a married gentleman in Staffordshire, and of Edward's hopes to obtain his university degree in June.

"You are fond of your family, Miss Billie."

"Yes, Your Grace. I am."

"And your parents, Sir Moreton and your mother, must be most proud of you. You are, perhaps, their favorite—yes? As the youngest, and the one daughter?"

"No, Your Grace." Billie could shake her head with some conviction. "I am not the favorite."

"Perhaps there is no favorite, then. As I am equally fond of all my grandsons." The comment reminded Billie that it was most certainly strange that, given the situation, David's *grand-mère* had not once mentioned his name or the supposed engagement.

All three ladies turned toward the hall door at the sound of new arrivals.

"I know that you know Hayden, Miss Billie, but perhaps your

aunt has not yet met my eldest grandson?" As the famously fair Marquis of Hayden entered the room, with his confident manner and dressed in his usual dark-garbed splendor, Billie read obvious affection in the duchess' gaze. But she read something else as well—a sadness, or a concern—that shadowed the elderly woman's welcoming smile.

"*Grand-mère,*" Hayden acknowledged, bowing gracefully before her and kissing her hand. He bowed to Billie and Ephie as well, then presented the two gentlemen accompanying him, Lord Knowles and Lord Demarest. "M'friend Gillen is due to be wed in a fortnight, ladies, and is runnin' about like a demented chicken, else I should have had the pleasure of presentin' him to you. And Demarest here has just announced his betrothal to Lady Constance. I swear these weddings and betrothals are a positive contagion! Soon I shan't have a single soul to whom to speak! I must rely upon my friend Knowles here to fill the gap. The *gap* with the *gape,* eh *grand-mère?*"

The company laughed. One could not spend more than a few days in town without hearing of Lord Knowles' loquacity. And indeed, Lord Knowles, taking no offense, proceeded to regale the company with the circumstances of Demarest's offer to Lady Constance, in such detail that Billie noticed that only Aunt Euphemia remained entranced.

"Miss Billie"—Hayden leaned close to address her—"will you step aside here a moment?" He was indicating one of the window embrasures, where the afternoon sun warmed an oak sill and highlighted the gold tassels upon the drapes. The window opened upon a small side garden alive with jonquils. As they stood apart, Hayden drew a letter from his watered-silk waistcoat. "I have been tasked"—he did not look at her but at the company as he handed Billie the sealed paper—"with delivering this."

Billie recognized the hand, with its direction to *Miss Caswell.* She had last seen that writing in January, but on heavier paper. She knew because she had kept the earlier note.

Quickly she broke the seal and read: *I shall be in town the first week in March. Will I see you? D. Trent*

Billie's lips firmed as she passed the open page, empty save for that one unsatisfactory line, back to Hayden.

"'Tis an outrageous waste of paper," she remarked. "And much too cryptic."

"Cryptic?" Hayden's eyebrows rose. "M'brother is invariably direct, Miss Caswell." He scanned the note, then looked up at her. "I rather think, Miss Billie, that you should comprehend that he sends you a *question*. It is up to *you* whether he sees you or not."

"He might more properly have asked, '*May* I see you?'"

"Ah, but David sometimes forgets to be proper." Hayden smiled. "And he never begs."

"Are you often your brother's interpreter?" she asked sharply.

"He has rarely needed one. But, yes, when he is inarticulate. As he seems to be lately."

She did not understand his look, and glanced away. Myles Trent, Marquis of Hayden, had always mystified her; she believed it too late to unravel him now.

"Perhaps," she ventured softly, as her gaze sought the other visitors, "he should also have tasked you with explaining why he left so abruptly in January."

"He is a soldier, Miss Caswell. No explanation is necessary."

"We are at peace. My brother Jack sold up last summer."

"How happy for him." At Hayden's ironic tone and slight bow, Billie's gaze was upon him once more.

"You would have me believe that *your* brother, *Lord* David, must 'soldier on'?"

"Certainly not. He follows his inclinations."

"Oh, that is too obvious! You might tell him for me, my lord, when you happen to see him, that I am determined he will *not* see me!"

Her temper merely drew a grin, and she left the alcove with a great deal of pride and no real satisfaction.

Two days later, on Saturday the fourth of March, Billie celebrated her nineteenth birthday with dancing and supper for almost sixty guests. She had little doubt that her imagined link to Lord David and the house of Braughton had much to do with the perfect attendance, because she simply had not been in town long enough to encourage many beyond a few old school friends. Thus, the group was a most curious mix of those few young misses from Mrs. Seton's boarding school, her brothers' variable acquaintance, and a range of younger ladies and some gentlemen in the charge of Aunt Euphemia's circle. That Lords Hayden, Demarest, Knowles, and several other pinks of the *ton* deigned to appear at short notice assured the gathering much-elevated cachet. Their presence could only feed the accepted speculation regarding Billie's prospects.

Lord Hayden's graceful presence in her home on such an occasion, and just after the coveted vouchers to Almack's had arrived, had sent Ephie into the boughs. Indeed, Billie suspected that her aunt's satisfaction had led her to forget the reason for hosting such a supper party—namely, her niece's birthday. Billie wondered wryly if she might slip away entirely, leaving the assemblage to bask in the Marquis of Hayden's splendor. Instead she moved on to another dance and watched anxiously for Kit's arrival. He had promised, to the extent that he was ever capable of promising, that he would not forget her birthday. But Kit had ever been Kit.

When her partner, the Earl of Windover, future brother-in-law to Lord Demarest, asked if anything were wrong, Billie forced herself to rally. She smiled as she denied any troubles at all, and was still making an effort to smile as Major Trent entered the doorway from the hall.

She missed the next step and immediately apologized. She had to rely upon Windover, a very skilled partner, to see her through the remainder of the dance, as her attention was so entirely fixed upon the unexpected scarlet coat and broad shoulders at the hall door. She could not meet David's gaze. But she felt the relief of knowing he was well.

Hayden had to have told him of the event, though it puzzled her that David should not have come with his brother's entourage. Had he just arrived? Billie's gaze at last sought his.

But he was speaking animatedly with two young ladies, two of Billie's newest acquaintances, May Sanders and Charis Athington. Billie did not truly feel at ease with either, but she was too new to town to be overly particular, and both were deemed excellent *ton*. May Sanders was an admired beauty— a petite blond who trailed a wake of suitors whatever the venue. Her friend, tall and elegantly stylish Charis Athington, was reputed to be the catch of the season—wealthy, lovely, and with every proper connection. The perfect Miss Athington was at that moment gazing raptly up into Major Trent's face.

Billie bit her lower lip.

"Miss Caswell." Lord Windover was frowning. "You are certain you are quite well? Perhaps we should sit out the rest of this set."

"No—no, my lord. This tune nears its end. I am only a bit thirsty. I shall take some punch at the break."

In truth she was parched. In truth, she felt she had been dancing for days without end. The room seemed very crowded and extremely hot, though all the fires had been lit earlier to ward off the pervasive March chill.

The dance ended. Billie thanked her patient partner. She wished only to escape into the empty supper room. But Kit had appeared from that very room—he must have entered the house from the mews—and now he handed Billie her much-desired glass of punch.

She thanked him and tried not to gulp the drink.

"When did you arrive?" she asked. "I've been watching—"
She realized she'd been watching only Major Trent.

"Came around back to surprise fusty old Withers and leave my gift for you in the kitchen."

"Whatever have you brought me?"

He laughed. "Come and see."

She was so relieved to have Kit sober, and to have an excuse to leave the party, that she let him lead her by the elbow through the drawing room and down to the kitchen. Cook and several startled servants abruptly ceased talking and looked at them in astonishment.

Kit left Billie's side to stride to the back door and open it to the cold night air. When he returned, he was holding a dripping, *moving* lobster above a copper pot.

"Look here, Billie! You love lobster patties—this fellow should give you a birthday feast!"

She had never seen a live lobster before. At once the thought of eating the magnificent, struggling creature made her ill.

Kit must have read the dismay on her face. "I won him off P.B. Marsh at Boodles this evening," he added stubbornly.

"*Won* him?"

"At faro. What's wrong, Billie? I thought you'd be pleased." He brought the poor thing closer. "Don't be squeamish, now. You used to like to find crayfish."

"Oh, Kit!" She fought the urge to wring her hands. It did seem that though everyone about him wished Kit would learn some sense, Kit himself was most determined to disappoint them. That he should bring such a thing to her party—and expect an ecstatic reception! Billie's gaze rather desperately sought out Cook's disapproving face.

"Not that way, Master Caswell," Cook cautioned as Kit moved to place the pot and the lobster on the stove. "We must boil the water first—else it will suffer."

"Suffer? Why, the thing's to be eaten!"

Kit was laughingly holding the lobster up to Cook's grim

features when a purposeful clearing of a throat at the kitchen door made Billie turn. Major Trent, looking every inch the distinguished military officer, his blue gaze focused in amusement on the scene before him, smartly bowed.

Billie knew she flushed, whether from embarrassment, the heat in the kitchen, or Lord David's quick, penetrating glance, she could not have said. She raised her chin, observing silently that he had at last managed to tear himself away from Charis Athington's charms.

"Your pardon," David said, apparently speaking most directly to Cook. "I was told I might find Miss Caswell in the kitchen." As his keen gaze took in Billie's pink cheeks, he seemed to be fighting a smile.

Kit's high spirits had fled. He again looked resentful.

"Why, *Major,*" he asked, "d'ya think my sister's preparing supper?"

"Certainly not, Mr. Caswell. You would appear to be the one charged with that chore."

"Oh, the devil!" Kit scornfully tossed the lobster into the midst of the carefully prepared serving dishes on the table. As Cook protested, Kit sent Billie a dark look. "One red back's as good as another, I s'pose," he muttered disagreeably, and he brushed rudely past Lord David, who stepped aside.

Recalling the major's charge that she "babied" her brother, Billie held her tongue. She had to concede that Kit had not acted just then in anything other than rag-mannered fashion.

"He is certainly a fine-looking young man," David conceded mildly. His gaze seemed to envelop her. "I had not seen him upright."

She almost rose to the bait, half compliment though it was. Instead she turned to Cook and assured herself that her brother's unusual and unfortunate gift would be handled appropriately. When she looked again toward the doorway, David Trent had held his ground. He still observed her closely. One might have suspected he had traveled all the way from the Continent for the express purpose of frequenting her aunt's kitchen.

"How kind of you to come, Major," she said, as she walked toward him.

"It is a major event." Despite his smile, despite his impeccable grooming and the dashing scarlet coat, he looked rather pale and tired. Billie fought her swift rise of concern. When she'd last seen him, at the New Year, she had released him; his welfare could be none of her affair.

"Did Lord Hayden convey my message?" she asked.

He smiled and shook his head. "Was it in answer to mine?"

"Yes."

"And was the answer yes?"

"No."

"Ah! But the question would now seem irrelevant—and how else shall I deliver your birthday present?" He did not step aside as she approached, as he had stepped aside for Kit, so that of necessity she came very near him. She was breathlessly aware of his height, of the scent of his shaving lotion, of how dark his pupils looked within the striking blue of his eyes. "I have missed you, Billie," he said softly.

"Have you? Is that why you have stayed away so long?"

"Does it seem long to you?"

She shook her head. As she mutely made to push past him, he at last moved aside and followed her into the dark stairwell. She could hear the laughter and music of the party in the rooms just overhead, and she stepped briskly toward the stairs. But a gentle pull on her arm stayed her at the very first step.

She turned to protest, only to find her face on a level with his.

"You said you wanted time," he continued softly. "How could I imagine you would object to more of it? Though I confess," he muttered, "it seems dreadfully long to me." And he swiftly kissed her.

For some seconds she forgot herself. Then she drew breath.

"You are too fond of kissing, Major."

"Perhaps because it is so rare."

"Surely you might determine whether it is rare or not?"

"No, Miss Caswell. You do." Again he smiled. "Though I fear you might reach the point that you feel you have had enough of my kisses—and devalue them. . . ."

"We shall never reach such a point!"

"I am pleased to hear it."

"That is not what I meant!" She had to think. His ready smile fascinated her.

"There must be no more kissing, though," he explained lightly, "until you have decided."

"I assure you, my lord, that is not a deprivation."

"I speak for myself, Billie." His gaze held hers. "Have you any news for me?"

With a strangled breath she managed only, "I shall not tryst here in the stairwell," and raced on up the steps.

For all she had been absent a good fifteen minutes, little about the gathering had changed. Except that May Sanders and Charis Athington were no longer occupied by dancing or conversation. Both girls were much too aware of her return with Major Trent; from across the parlor, they boldly assessed the major at her side. Billie took the happy group into dazed, uncomprehending view all at once—because she felt so closely the presence of her partner. Everyone at this party believed her engaged to him, yet in all these weeks she had received not one word from him, not of love or even of liking. They ought to deny any intention here, now, finally and openly. But he had kissed her once again. . . .

"Will you not go?" she urged under her breath, sensing only that she could not manage both the major and the party at once. "This is not the time to talk. I do not want you here." She knew instantly that she'd been too sharp. To treat him so was disgraceful. When she glanced at him, his fine jaw had set stubbornly. She swallowed. "I mean you—you must of course stay for some supper. As you have come all this way . . ."

"I think not," he said abruptly. She had never seen him look quite so stern. He was signaling the butler for his coat and hat. "As you say, I have indeed come a long way—from the Channel and Dover through the night—and would benefit from some sleep." As he shrugged into his high-collared greatcoat, he drew a small parcel, carefully wrapped in paper and twine, from one deep pocket. "Happy Birthday, Miss Caswell," he said, tendering it to her without a smile. " 'Tis from Brittany. On seeing it, I thought of you and your brothers." He did not meet her gaze as he bowed and swiftly exited, letting in a rush of frigid air at the door.

Only later, when the company had left and the house was silent, when she could most self-indulgently regret rejecting his company, did Billie unwrap the perfect Faience pottery box with its charming depiction of one skirted girl amid a host of boys.

Chapter Five

"We've the devil to pay," Hayden muttered, as David stood next to him at the following Monday's musicale. The angry cries from the street outside were much at variance with the politely restrained evening in progress indoors. Their hostess, the mother of pretty May Sanders, could never have reckoned on the circumstances in town that night.

With the introduction in Parliament of the Corn Importation Law, a bill calculated to keep grain prices high and the pockets of wealthy landowners full, much of the poorer populace of the countryside appeared to have descended on the capital to object. Deliberations on the bill in the Commons had begun only that morning, and tempers both on the floor and out on the street were running hot.

David reflected that the weekend had certainly not been an auspicious one on which to return to London. He had left behind a continent at peace, only to confront an armed camp in the West End.

Since his return, he had scarcely seen his brother, Hayden, catching only a brief glimpse of him two nights before, at Billie Caswell's birthday party. And because *Grand-mère* had wanted David to reside not at Hayden's rooms in St. James's but with her at the town house, there had been little opportunity to speak.

At this evening's informal recital, they were meant to be listening to May Sanders play the harp. May Sanders herself

had invited him. But David's attention had been drawn instead
to the back of Billie Caswell's glossy head. She sat among the
attentive audience, as immovably courteous as most, though—
because she sat at the end of the row—he could see the slight
impatient tapping of her gloved fingers against her lap.

To distract himself he whispered to Hayden, "How shall
Father vote on the bill?" The duke usually took Hayden's recommendation. "That is, if the thing should pass?"

"Oh, it will pass. Nothing more certain than that this rush
to remedy should pass."

"And then how shall Father vote?"

"Why, as he's always voted." Hayden eyed him languidly,
then returned his attention to the musicians. "In his own interest!
But if you are asking if the Lords will then approve the bill—
that is a surety as well." He sighed. "If I troubled to counsel
anything, 'twould be delay. 'Tis all an unseemly hurry to tin-
ker. We might reasonably wait a year or more to see how the
peace suits. But I shan't trouble." He straightened a coat
sleeve, as though matters of state were, after all, of trifling import.

"These mobs grow surly," David observed. "I sailed across
from Calais with Lord Castlereagh's suite. The folk meeting
us at Dover seemed cheerful enough. But as we came on to
London, the dissent increased. I feared some wished him
physical harm."

"Naturally the discontents must focus their ire on the For-
eign Secretary—no matter that he's been away in Vienna. The
issue is certainly on his plate now." He looked at David. "Why
did you not stay in France, to go on to Vienna with Wellington? D'you plan to cash out after all? Or were you concerned
about the filly?"

"I wish you would not refer to Miss Caswell so, Myles."

"Why, 'twas you yourself likened her to your horse! At the
New Year."

"I shouldn't have done so. The color of her hair put me in

mind of it, that is all." David's gaze drifted again to that dark chestnut head. "And I like to watch her walk."

"Walk?"

"Yes. She's most graceful, yet assured. She has no fear."

"Even *I* have *some* fears, David."

"And it shows in your walk."

Myles promptly and surreptitiously elbowed him, a hard jab that might easily have toppled him. But David held his place.

"In all seriousness, Myles," he whispered. "I must have a decision from her—if not tonight, then soon. I had no interest in moving on to Vienna with Wellington; I've no taste for diplomacy. Either I rejoin the regiment or sell up and head home."

"You were always one for doin' and rushin' about. Perhaps you ought to stand for this energetic Parliament." But Hayden sobered as he listened to May Sanders pluck dutifully upon her harp. "I've mentioned before that Father wants you home. And nothing would please *Grand-mère* more than if you were to skip off to Scotland with Miss Billie—and promise her a great-grandchild."

"*Grand-mère* would be even more pleased were *you* to marry."

Hayden shook his head. "I am incapable of pleasing her."

"*Au contraire.* You are the one most capable of pleasing her. But you are also the least inclined to do so."

The Marquis of Hayden had no response. Since David knew he had simply stated the truth, he did not refine upon it. So much of what *Grand-mère* had said to him and to his cousin Chas in the past year had evidenced her frustration over Hayden's apparent apathy. One did not fret so if one did not care very much indeed.

May Sanders finished her ordeal. Before the next performer, a young lady whose complexion defiantly challenged her pink gown, could be prevailed upon to leave the safety of her seat, Charis Athington was up out of her own—and rather too obviously and playfully importuning Billie Caswell to seek the stage. Billie was shaking her bright head.

"Egad! We can't have that, can we?" Hayden observed with a wince. "Will you not intervene?"

David smiled and declined. With a disgusted sigh, Hayden moved as though to leave the room.

"Do stay, Myles." David put a hand on his brother's sleeve. "I'll wager she'll surprise us all. Or if not, 'twill be worth it to watch her brazen it out."

"You would let the girl be embarrassed? That is clearly Athington's aim."

"I do not expect Miss Caswell to be embarrassed."

"You act as though she is your pet."

"No." David followed Billie's progress as she made her way to the piano. "But I am proud of her."

Billie did not appear in the least flustered; instead she looked thoughtful, as though she silently reviewed her repertoire of possible pieces. David did not miss the expression on Charis Athington's face. Despite the spoiled beauty's evident intention, despite her anticipation, David thought Charis destined to be disappointed.

Even as he thought it, Charis sent him a sly, sidelong glance. David quickly looked to the piano.

"What do you think of the Misses Sanders and Athington?" he asked Hayden softly.

"Ah, Miss Sanders—the pocket Venus." Hayden quizzed golden-haired May with his glass. "So petite and prettily packaged—with no room left for a heart. And the elegant Miss Athington—of the dark eyes and sharp tongue. . . . She is known to be very hard on a fella." He dropped his glass and glanced at David. "I hear they dance well," he conceded.

David stifled a laugh. "I should have guessed you would not be entranced."

Myles acknowledged that with a tilt of his head. "You

understand, then," he whispered as Billie began to play, "why I remain fancy-free."

Billie had chosen Bach, a short but difficult prelude. Though David had guessed at her proficiency, he was still pleasantly surprised. Her rendition was far from a simple exercise; there was nothing tired or methodical about the crisp clarity of the music, nothing merely competent about her playing. Though he could not recall much of the piece, David knew she played it both accurately and beautifully. And the choice was appropriate, fitting the evening's effort at entertainment more comfortably than any lengthy, virtuosic display.

She had said she'd been compelled to learn piano, but clearly she had also learned to love it, for her performance sparkled. No one among the company even dared cough while she played, and once she finished, the clapping was heartfelt rather than perfunctory. As Billie smiled, Charis Athington looked stony. Billie was prevailed upon to continue with an encore, a charming and much too brief sample of Gluck that David had never before heard for solo piano. He wondered if Billie might even have transcribed the number herself.

"How did you know?" Hayden asked, as Billie met with renewed applause.

David shrugged. "I simply trust in Miss Billie."

Hayden's gaze measured him. "You are in love with her," he said simply.

David let the accusation stand. He'd suspected as much when he'd acted like a smitten schoolboy in the stairwell the other night. Though his thoughts had dwelled most exclusively on Wilhelmina Caswell the past two months, he'd not until that moment considered that he might indeed be in love with his fiancée. After all, he had imagined himself in love half a dozen times; he had never suffered before. The symptoms, though severe, were not yet so debilitating. . . .

"I am aware though, Myles," he said softly, "that she must

choose me. Not in the idolizing manner of the sprout she once was. But as the young woman she now is. And further, I find I honor and admire the lady too much. Too much to believe that I might truly be her best choice."

Myles was silent for some time. "As you are already betrothed," he said at last, "I would suggest you wed her, then woo her. You might persuade her to the proper choice later. 'Tis not the time to gamble or to think overmuch about it."

David shook his head. "I haven't your liking for such games."

"You never did," Hayden conceded with a shrug. "But they do serve their purpose."

"Miss Caswell and I have been conducting all in reverse, Myles—putting a betrothal before a courtship, for one. So ludicrously, in fact, that I think the business must end. I mustn't take advantage. She has worries enough with that family."

"Then you must simply adopt the lot of them. I've always pictured you with a brood of children, dogs, and in-laws—though not in that order, of course. For one of your vaunted good nature, such a household might prove suitably trying."

David was not inclined to smile. "Her brother Kit is trouble," he acknowledged, "an indulged sprig who quickly grows tiresome. Whatever the source of his resentments, I now seem to be their object. He needs to have some manners drilled into him. But as for his apparent lack of sense—" He broke off with a heavy sigh.

"Young Caswell hangs about with Dumont."

"Ronald Dumont?" David asked in surprise. "Is Kit gambling heavily, then?"

"I s'pose 'heavily' depends on his resources. Sir Moreton Caswell has deep pockets. Your young Wilhelmina has a sizeable portion. Did you not know?"

David abruptly shut his astonished mouth. "I did not."

"Perhaps you will take my advice then and run off with her tonight."

"I thought you counseled delay rather than 'rushing about.' "
Hayden's smile was broad. "Not once the bet is on the table."

This time David did laugh, too distinctly. Though no young lady was then exhibiting her skills, enough of the audience turned reprovingly toward them to alert David to his transgression. For the first time that evening Billie Caswell looked directly at him. Though she glanced only briefly over her shoulder, he was fully aware of her penetrating, amber-brown gaze. Her look, her whole manner, conveyed that she thought him rude. His jaw set. He had been listening so very patiently to everyone besides Billie Caswell, who was the only performer he had cared to hear.

She had once more presented her back to him. He noted again that she had dressed her hair very prettily that evening, gathered to the back of her head, then let to fall in lustrous ringlets upon her nape and shoulders. He was glad she had not yielded to cropping her hair in the fashionable style. He had the unwelcome, possessive urge to kiss her shoulder—an urge that he would have preferred not to fight. He concentrated very hard on the duo now on view. The girl in pink was too tentatively singing a ballad, to the accompaniment of a sour-faced governess' mandolin. Outside, what sounded like an increasingly agitated crowd repeatedly shouted, "No Corn Laws!"

The protestors' noise was overwhelming the performance inside. David watched more than one distracted head turn in the direction of the street.

"I wonder they do not call out the Guard," he whispered to Hayden.

"They must. I cannot stay in any event, as I—"

An angry pounding at the house next door interrupted him. The pounding yielded to louder cries against the Corn Laws, then the sharp sound of shattering glass. The performance halted.

Mrs. Sanders, their dismayed hostess, could not keep her

voice level as she gasped out, "Do, pray, keep your seats! 'Tis for Mr. Harknett next door, who stands for Bexbridge. He'll vote—" She screamed as one of the casement windows in their salon suddenly smashed into bits. A good-sized brick landed with a thud on the shard-covered carpet between David and Billie Caswell.

As the rest of the panicked guests shrieked and scrambled across the chairs to the opposite side of the room, Billie whirled to face the disturbance.

For an amazed second, David observed her slim, steady form. One man in a thousand might have turned in like manner to confront a threat. That a slip of a girl should do so without flinching took his breath.

In two long strides he'd reached her and swept her up into his arms. She was too startled to protest as he sped with her to the safety of a corner.

"Fool," he breathed, as much to himself as to her as he released her. He retained a hold on her shoulders, pulling her tightly against his side. An empty bottle followed the brick through the broken window, to crack against the toppled chairs just ahead of Billie's former seat.

The chant from the crowd had gained strength, occasionally rising into a series of cries as the mass of protestors swelled and surged. Billie's aunt Euphemia, her hands fluttering nervously before her, made her way haltingly from a far corner of the room.

"Billie!" she said, her voice atremble. But her gaze focused pointedly on David's close grasp. "Are you quite all right?"

David dropped his arm to permit Billie to step away from him.

"Quite all right, Ephie," Billie said. She looked up then into David's face. "Why did you do that?"

"*Why?* Because your unreasoned impulse, though likely qualifying as brave, might well have killed you!"

"And *your* 'unreasoned impulse'?"

He thought her eyes very large and dark. The spots of color in her cheeks only heightened their brilliance.

"My pleasure, I assure you, Miss Caswell." As he bowed to her, he felt her gaze upon his lowered head. That she should fault him, that she should remain so distant, grated immeasurably. Had he not saved her?

The rooms were rather dim, as the draft through the broken window had blown out a good many candles. The yells and huzzaing from the street were constant, and now—in the absence of music and the flimsy barrier of glass—their tenor and import were clear. The riot still threatened. In such anger and confusion, anyone's house might be targeted. David thought it imperative to move the Sanderses' guests to the safety of the inner rooms.

Turning away from Billie, he spoke to Hayden, requesting his aid in removing guests to the hall, a request with which Hayden promptly complied—as though the marquis were used to taking orders from his younger brother.

David directed two trembling servants to douse the remaining candles in the drawing room, then strode toward one huddled group of guests on the far side of the salon. As he passed in front of the windows, he could see the angry mob lit by street lanterns outside. A section of the neighbor's front iron fencing had been torn up, to be carried aloft like a trophy.

As he herded half a dozen women toward the relative safety of the hallway, he noticed, with a lack of surprise, that his brother had managed, in his inimitable fashion, to coax most of the other anxious guests into a quiet, orderly arrangement. David also noticed, with less satisfaction, that Charis Athington and May Sanders had positioned themselves next to Billie Caswell.

He did not trust himself to look directly at Billie.

"What do you anticipate, Major?" Charis asked in a tone more excited than fearful. "Are we to be invaded?"

"I do not know, Miss Athington. But here we are at least

removed from further missiles and might exit front or back, as need be."

"How glad I am to have you here with me!" And Charis Athington's hand sought his sleeve. For a second David stared in astonishment at her extremely feminine, and extremely forward, fingers. When he glanced up at Billie, he met an accusing glare. Then she turned her face away, presenting him with only a profile—and an elevated one at that.

"Oh, Charis! Mama has fainted!" And oblivious to the flirtatious interests of Miss Athington, May Sanders abruptly pulled her friend along with her to attend her swooning parent.

Though his arm was now free, David noted that Billie's face remained averted. As Miss Euphemia Caswell stood ready to keep her niece company, David left them and wended his way through the huddled guests. Hayden was leaning nonchalantly against the expensive Chinese paper in the dark hall. It was incongruous to see him thus, with so many nervous, whispering females fluttering about him, the scent of reviving *sal volatile* pervasive, and so few other gentlemen present. Even Mr. Sanders had not been prevailed upon to attend his own daughter's recital that evening.

"Are you armed?" Hayden asked under his breath.

"No." Something about his brother's expression prompted David to counter, "Are you?" With Hayden's answering grin, he exclaimed, "Good lord, Myles—at a ladies' musicale?"

Hayden shrugged. "I knew how events progressed. One cannot be too cautious. I'd venture to say the gleam in Miss Athington's eye should have put any man *en garde*."

In other circumstances David would have laughed. But he ignored the reference to Charis Athington and looked instead toward Billie. He could just discern her white-gowned form beside the drawing room doorway. That he should feel the bond with her, a close, unacknowledged connection, was a revelation. He should not be dwelling on *her* in this instance, only acting.

"If your carriage is still in back, Myles, I would ask you to see the Misses Caswell home. I feel I must remain here with our hostess until this mob has moved on. But I find it—I find it distracting that I cannot trust her—Miss Billie, that is, not to—" He knew he was babbling and abruptly stopped. He simply did not want Billie Caswell harmed.

"Let me check the back," Hayden offered. "With luck we might evacuate most of this lot without ill effect."

After Hayden left, David reentered the abandoned salon and quickly pulled the drapes shut. From one hidden side of a window recess he discreetly surveyed the throng in the street as it milled about, yelling and cheering. Every so often another shout of "No Corn Laws!" could be discerned amid the noise. A window in a house to the east cracked at another projectile. But to his practiced eye the drift of the crowd was now away from the Sanderses' town house.

Hayden met him as he returned to the hall. "My good coachman, Perkins, had the sense to lay to in an alley a block away," he said, "along with Leigh-Maitland's carriage and driver."

"Then would you consider offering to take Miss Athington and her mama up with you as well?"

"Gladly. And as Lady Grimstock's equipage has run off, I shall invite that vigilant lady to accompany us."

David knew that Hayden would only endure Lady Grimstock's company in his own interest. No better protection from Charis Athington than coldly correct Lady Grimstock!

"If Leigh-Maitland takes more of the female contingent with him, we might significantly reduce the party here," Hayden added. "You will still stay?"

David nodded. "Mrs. Sanders is overset. Though I hear cries that the Guards approach, I would see them before leaving. As it is, anyone might come through the windows."

He watched Myles cross to Billie and escort her and her aunt toward the back of the hall. When Billie briefly glanced

David's way, he attempted a small smile, which he suspected she could not see—or did not choose to.

The roar from the street was dissipating. David opened the front door to find the Guard now clearing the crowd before them. With that development, he sent the overwrought Mrs. Sanders and her daughter safely upstairs to rest, then dispatched a manservant for a carpenter and glazier. He pressed more servants to locate blankets to hang upon the drapery rods in the drawing room against the chill of the night. He escorted two parties of relieved guests out back, where several constables had arrived to shepherd them home. Upon Mr. Sanders' return an hour later, David at last walked back alone to his *grand-mère*'s, to find a supper of soup and bread in the kitchen and a scribbled note from Hayden: *Miss Billie requests, 'When all is calmer—when he is able—would you ask him please to come to me?'*

And David knew she had at last made her decision.

Chapter Six

The week was a miserable one. When Billie recalled what she had heard of the previous season's pleasures, she wondered what whimsical fate had determined that her own come-out should occur during such a decidedly unsettled spring. In the streets, railing and rioting against the Corn Bill had consumed the previous three days, leading to damaged property, countless injuries, and even several deaths. Throughout the West End a pervasive air of nervous tension never eased. And from all reports, the discussions in Parliament over the proposal were almost as violent as the crowds outside. In light of such tumult, fretting over society's cancelled engagements had seemed frivolous in the extreme.

Billie knew that her mood echoed the agitation in town. She had secretly been delighted by Lord David's appearance at both her birthday evening and the Sanderses' musicale, but she could not rid herself of a pronounced melancholy. Though for years she had anticipated happiness in achieving her heart's aim, in obtaining the attentions of Lord David, she instead felt little—as though she had taken advantage, as though she had not been quite sporting. Yes, at the Braughton New Year's gala, Lord David had maneuvered her to that secluded alcove, but she had wanted to go. And though everything about him had signaled his intention to kiss her, she had made no move to flee. She still considered she had trapped him, and in trapping him, herself.

Her honor, her belief in fair play, demanded that she release him from all obligation, that she remove any claim her family had upon the house of Braughton and David Trent. The major had not taken her seriously in January—perhaps rightly, since her refusal then had been so tempestuously delivered. With time, she herself had thought her reaction excessive. In any event, their fathers had not abandoned their hopes for a union; they still thought their offspring intended for each other. Billie wished now only to relieve her own sense of guilty oppression; the "getting" of David Trent had not proved as satisfying as she had always imagined. She could not bear the sly smiles and speculative asides of May Sanders and Charis Athington. If the idea of a betrothal were openly denied, Billie thought she might still find some noble, lonely enjoyment in the season.

Yet he was apparently ignoring her request that he come to see her.

Billie tried to concentrate on her needlework as she and her aunt awaited callers. Sewing was one of Billie's least favorite occupations; she knew Ephie heard her frustrated sighs with answering, silent reproof. That afternoon Billie might almost have preferred the arrival of Kit and the necessity to confront yet another of his increasingly rash and troubling starts. A sorry state indeed, she thought—pricking her finger once again—that she should long for another of Kit's disasters as entertainment.

They were soon, thankfully, treated to company—in the form of Lord Grenby, whose marked attentions to Billie were becoming more frequent. Several other young gentlemen, perhaps aware of Major Lord David Trent's prior claim, tended to hover with sheepish looks and irritating hesitance. The season's misses, given fears for their safety in the streets that week, had been venturing out infrequently. But Billie and Ephie had paid some calls the previous day, and that afternoon they were rewarded in turn. Yet as the afternoon advanced, and despite the full drawing room, Billie despaired of ever seeing Major Trent again. When Charis Athington arrived, to quiz her yet again regarding the nonexistent betrothal, Billie found it impossible to remain composed.

"I assure you, Miss Athington," she snapped as Charis cornered her over the seed cake, "it is all unfounded. A complete hum."

"We should not be anticipating the announcement any day, then?" Charis' dark eyes glittered speculatively.

"No."

"Then—pardon me, Miss Caswell—but if there is no real affection in the case and no hope for an attachment, you might inform the rest of us. Perhaps then we might . . . try our own fortunes?" Though Charis' tone was light, Billie thought the comment far from playful. And as determined as she had been to end all chatter about an engagement, she was tempted to direct Charis Athington elsewhere.

"I suspect Major Trent would be most happy to entertain you," she managed instead, while privately hoping that David would have the good sense to send Charis off about other business.

Major Trent had the pleasure of encountering the departing Miss Athington just as he himself was announced. Billie watched the two briefly exchanging words, then watched David bend low over Charis' hand. Billie thought it likely that Charis would find an excuse to delay her departure. Abruptly turning her back upon the two, Billie beamed upon a delighted Lord Grenby. But she was aware of David's approach—just behind her left shoulder—even before he spoke.

"Grenby," he acknowledged. "How d'you do?"

"Lord David." And Grenby graciously bowed. But he was quick to excuse himself. "I will not intrude upon your time with Miss Caswell."

The major's presence, or perhaps Grenby's departure, appeared to signal the rest of the company, for Billie was immediately flooded with well-wishes and adieus, until—after scarcely more than five minutes—she and Major Trent were left alone with Ephie.

"Should you like some refreshment, Major?" Ephie asked, making—at least as it seemed to Billie—an excess of bustle and noise with the china.

"No, thank you, Miss Caswell. I have all I might desire." At that Ephie smiled benignly and settled herself once again to embroider. Though her aunt now sat at the far end of the hearth, Billie fervently wished her even farther.

"You look lovely, Miss Billie," Lord David said, at once drawing her attention from her aunt. Her gaze met his with the recognition that he always seemed curiously familiar, as though he had simply stepped away for an hour or two, though the interval might have been months. "What would you call this color?" he asked, as her bemused gaze focused on his gesturing hand. "The color of your sash?"

"Blue," she said, instantly aware that that would not do, just as the simple word *blue* could never quite describe his eyes.

Lord David's smile actually reached those eyes.

"I had thought the drapers more imaginative," he remarked. "Surely it must be called 'ocean' or 'sea mist'?" As he held her look, Billie wished she might avoid this conversation—though she had been anticipating it for some weeks.

"Major . . ." she began, only to see him shake his head.

"I think it should be David now. As we are such . . . old friends."

"Perhaps you ought to hear me first," she said.

And at that rather ominous caution, his look sobered. "I must compliment you, Miss Caswell, on your performance the other night—both at the piano and in the face of considerable danger."

"You called me a fool."

"Just so." He shrugged. "All bravery is foolish. But only one man in a thousand would have stood his ground as you did, untrained."

"Oh, but I am trained, Major," she admitted easily. "All of my life, I've had to force myself—always—to match my brothers for boldness. Indeed, sometimes to exceed them."

"Whatever its basis, 'tis bravery." He smiled. "I should prefer ten of you to a battalion."

She swallowed, suspecting she had never before been more highly complimented.

"I have not thanked you," she managed, "for the lovely porcelain box. It is charming and does indeed remind me of my brothers. 'Twas thoughtful of you to bring it so far."

Again he shrugged. "Paris no longer seems far. As I mentioned, I was struck by the figures. Your brothers mean much to you, and you are very good to them." His gaze assessed her. "I've encountered Mr. Morty occasionally in town this past week. But he did not attend the musicale?"

"No. He—he seems to have fixed his interest on a certain young lady. She is also just out this season—Esther Urquhart?" As he shook his head, Billie feared she threatened to bore him; the season's debutantes could not be of the slightest interest to him. Except, of course, for Miss Athington.

"And your youngest brother, Edward? I have not seen him since the New Year."

"Edward will be joining us here soon, for end of term, at Easter." There was a silence as Christopher's whereabouts and activities went unacknowledged. Kit's rudeness in the kitchen at her birthday was only the least of Billie's concerns. She thought it likely that Kit's heavy wagers had come to David's notice, as the *ton* seemed most eager to broadcast all. "My brother Jack writes that he will soon make me an aunt," she relayed instead, and as brightly as possible.

"My compliments to him," David said. "He sold out when?"

"Last May. Almost a year ago." The opening was one she

could not ignore. "Do you—do you intend now to relinquish your commission, Major?"

His relief was almost palpable.

"You must determine it, Miss Caswell," he said with a smile. "In January you released me. I grant I'd been unforgivably rude. But given the uncertain circumstances—there at the doorstep—and since you have not alerted your father, or—I should say—since he has not alerted *mine*—they still have their hopes."

Whatever courage he had found to commend in her seemed to have deserted her. Billie's gaze took in his striking uniform, with its bright red wool and elaborate braided epaulets.

"Sometimes," he continued softly, observing her, "a decision, any decision, is the only requirement. I should like one now—yes, no, or that you must have more time."

Billie swallowed. She did not truly wish to say no, but she could not condemn him to yes. And she could not ask again for more time; doing so would delay the decision he deserved. The major wished to be getting on.

"No," she said.

His smile held. But something of humor fled his gaze. Billie suspected that no man could enjoy being refused, whatever the relief of it. She sensed also that no matter what she said, their connection was accepted, a given. There had always been an undercurrent that defied words.

"You think we would not suit?" he asked lightly.

"That is not the point."

"It is very much the point!" But he checked himself and partly turned from her. "I suppose it says a great deal about my vanity—that had you said yes, I would not have sought the reasons. But as you've told me no, and as we've always spoken openly with each other, perhaps you might share your reasons with me now? Despite your dismissal in January, I confess I'd expected to send an announcement to the *Times*."

She thought her jaw might actually have dropped. She'd

had no notion he was so committed. But he had asked for an explanation. . . .

"First, then—the circumstances are not at all conducive to any . . . any lasting contentment. You should not—that is, *we* should not be held accountable for a moment's indiscretion. 'Tis not . . . *enlightened.*" As his eyes widened, she added, "I am certain that if either of us could return to the New Year, we would not repeat the mistake. That alone is in the nature of a test—repentance."

He looked amused. "I assure you, Miss Billie, my thoughts have returned to the New Year quite often indeed, and with too much pleasure to believe myself at all repentant." As she blushed, he went on. "You cite the 'circumstances' that bound us as something entirely negative. But could they not also be an opportunity?"

"How do you mean, Major?"

"Why, that we established that we like each other well enough—before the interference of our fathers. And we are neighbors—an unexpected boon, as I'd thought to have my cousin Chas, who has an exceptional eye, pick out a promising piece of ground for me near Braughton. The timing would seem opportune as well, for if I were not selling out and settling down just now, I should probably be looking to rejoin my regiment."

"The House Guards—the Coldstream regiment."

"Yes." He smiled. "You spoke of the 'circumstances' as your first reason. Is there another?"

She nodded. "My family. My brothers. You know that you do not get on—"

"Get on!"

She thought he held back a laugh.

"My dear Miss Billie, any group of men would 'get on' with considerably less inducement than *your* contentment." His easy gallantry again made her blush. "I assure you, we would find a way to do it."

"You do not understand! Kit is now in—he is now in very deep. With gentlemen like P.B. Marsh and Ronald Dumont."

"Mr. Christopher does not appear to think very clearly—if he thinks at all."

She set her shoulders. "That is precisely the kind of comment I find objectionable!"

"It is a fact. I have advised you before, Miss Billie, that you should not distress yourself by taking any responsibility for the folly of your brother."

"You choose to be cavalier, to be too dismissive. Would you not come to the aid of your own brother, Lord Hayden? He has certainly come to yours."

"As you are so enamored of my brother, perhaps you should much prefer to marry *him*."

"You move too quickly to something absurd! It is astonishing! What has Lord Hayden to do with anything?"

"What has Christopher Caswell?"

She glared at him. "You asked for my reasons, Major. I think perhaps I should not continue."

"You mean there are more?" He appeared to realize he had sounded rude, and briefly firmed his lips. "Let me simply say first, that with regard to your brothers, there is every chance I might in time grow to like them rather well. I share interests with Edward—once I can master my envy that he might spend his days reading. And apparently I share some experience with your absent brother, the captain. With Morty"—he paused and lifted his chin as though his collar chafed—"that may take some time. But perhaps if he were to find contentment with Miss Urquhart, he might forgive me my ancient trespass with Cora Peebles."

Wishing to hide her smile, Billie glanced quickly at the fire.

"As for Kit," he continued, "someday you must enlighten me as to why he holds me in such dislike."

"Oh, that. I suspect Kit envies you. He had a great desire to purchase colors, and my parents would not allow it. My mother would not even permit Kit to join the local militia. Not while Jack was with the regulars. And after Jack sold out, with the peace, Kit lost interest. Yes, I think, Major, that he must envy you your adventures."

" 'Twould be an independence gained at considerable cost. I have mentioned as much before."

"Yes. But surely you understand it?"

He nodded. His gaze examined her closely. "I believe he may also be jealous of *your* attentions, Miss Billie. Perhaps he objects to the fact that I . . . distract you in any fashion."

"If that were the case"—she smiled—"one might believe I would have more influence over him. But I appear to have little." She sighed. "I cannot keep him from his gaming."

The room had grown darker. The evening had set in. Aunt Ephie still sat absorbed by her stitching at the hearth. Billie wondered when the lamps had been lit; she had not noticed. She thought it would have been welcome, and so very comfortable, to sit with David Trent and plan a future by firelight. But instead of gratifying her heart's desire, she meant to defeat it.

"You said you had more reasons," he prompted, "for sending me on my way?"

"Yes, I—" She lowered her voice, not wishing Ephie to hear. "I cannot help but notice your attentions to Miss Athington. I would not keep you from pursuing such an interest."

To her astonishment, he laughed. "Attentions to Miss Athington!" he protested. "But that is nonsense! I have no interest in Miss Athington. 'Tis not chivalrous to say so, I know, but the 'attentions' have all been on her part. My interest has been in you alone."

She swallowed. "But who knows who else might have drawn your interest, had you not found yourself obligated to me?"

"That is a different argument and one I cannot address, as it falls so entirely within the realm of conjecture. I did not set out with the notion of marrying this spring, Miss Billie. Indeed, I'd had little time for entertaining the idea. But any concerns for Miss Athington's sensibilities are misplaced. Again, I know I am not charitable, but my observation has been that May Sanders and Charis Athington should not be counted among your friends."

"Because they are yours?"

For a moment he was silent, and rather white about the mouth. She hadn't meant to provoke him so; his readiness to refute her had surprised her. Surely he had to be relieved that she cried off? She wondered why the man could not simply be grateful for her understanding and be done with it.

"That those two should be *your* friends, Miss Billie, surprises me," he said loftily. "Because they are everything you are not—vain, designing, and mean-spirited."

He had again complimented her—rather grandly, as it happened—but she scarcely had a second to enjoy what he'd said, before he was adding, "If these are your reasons, I confess I do not find them insurmountable. I am still prepared to honor the arrangement."

" 'Prepared'! My lord, I have tried every way I might to make clear that I do not seek such a sacrifice from you! 'Prepared'? Is that why you persist, and present yourself with all your braid glittering before my eye—because you treat this as a campaign? I suppose it has not occurred to you that I—I wish to be free?"

She had never before seen him look so put out, not even at the New Year's unmasking. And, amazingly, his temper registered entirely in his gaze. Those striking blue eyes were suddenly darker and startlingly cold.

"*That* is another matter. You might have said so at once. I'd have found your interest in entertaining Lord Grenby, or some other nod-head, far more plausible than your ostensible *reasons*."

"You—you know you wish to be released as well."

"You mistake me." His searching gaze was difficult to bear. "Is this punishment, then, for having been too forward?"

"It is not a punishment."

"Oh, but it is," he said darkly. Abruptly he bowed, very gracefully and correctly. "Obliged to you, Miss Caswell. Miss Caswell." He nodded to Ephie. "I shall expect Sir Moreton to be informed." And while Billie still stood shaking, he left the room. Seconds later, the front door closed heavily.

Billie stepped closer to the fire. Leaning one hand against the mantel, she closed her eyes. The flames seemed to be giving off very little heat; she felt unexpectedly chilled. She had never thought to see smiling, teasing, laughing David Trent so grim. Yet surely his pride would recover shortly, and then he would know himself grateful.

"Well . . ." Ephie said, reminding Billie of their silent audience. "I have always thought you a remarkably sensible girl. Indeed, how could you be otherwise, with all those brothers? And so honest and frank." Busying herself in storing her sewing, Ephie still had not looked up. "I've long known you'd prefer half a dozen pursuits to tattling with debutantes or hemming a stitch. Indeed, why should you be pressed to such frippery, given your unusual maturity and wisdom?" Ephie's sharp brown gaze rose to meet hers accusingly. "But when a man takes the time to be as candid as the major was just now with you, and you haven't the good sense to value it—well, Miss Wilhelmina! I'll warrant you'll not find another like him!"

"I don't expect to, Ephie," she said wearily. Oddly, having released him from his pledge, she *felt* the pledge all the more.

"He has offered twice now, Billie. Do you anticipate he shall offer again?"

"I don't know, Aunt. I would hope, after this, that he shan't."

"The more fool you! I know you, Billie. You probably believe you have acted in fairness. But 'tis a misplaced sense of fairness you have—as though you both play at some sport!

The rules to which you take such exception were meant to protect just such as you. And they protect the gentlemen as well. Did it not occur to you that the major might now find himself held up to ridicule? In any event, you are unlikely to find the *ton* half as warm as it has been."

"*He* needn't be ridiculed. *He* did not cry off. And nothing was announced, nothing was agreed upon—there were no settlements. I have injured only myself."

"You think that, do you? And what if he cared for you? The two of you certainly bicker as though you were very close indeed." Billie stood silently as Ephie's lips pursed. "You had best hope he regains his equanimity," she offered sternly, "and trots back here again tomorrow."

But the next morning brought the news that Napoleon Bonaparte, having escaped his confinement on the island of Elba, had landed on the south coast of France and meant to make his triumphant way back to Paris. Billie knew then that if Major Lord David were to be "trotting back" anywhere, it would most likely be to renewed conflict on the Continent, and not to her own chilly doorstep.

Chapter Seven

She had released him; he did not feel released. Yet he would have to go—he wished to go. As soon as he heard the news, David knew he would be off to Brussels, where the army remained. He did not trouble to reflect on whether he'd have felt honor-bound to stay for Billie Caswell had she wished to wed; she had said no, and the matter was ended. Though last night, even in his spurned state, he had still thought to renew his offer at some later date, he now suspected any such effort would have to be postponed until very much later indeed. Wellington would need every soldier at hand—he would have difficulties enough finding experience at such short notice. The most seasoned regiments, veterans of the Peninsular campaign, were not yet back from America. Others with experience had been demobilized or had chosen half pay and gardening in the counties.

The rest of the army was near Brussels, and Wellington, who had just taken up the post of Ambassador to the Congress of Vienna, would be turning right around to reach his forces.

There was no question in David's mind that Wellington would be entreated once more to lead Britain and the allies. There was also no question that Parliament would vote for war. Bonaparte had not stayed caged on Elba—he would not stay caged within France. He could not be trusted to live at peace with his former enemies.

David supposed it fortuitous that the Congress still met in

Vienna, assuring a quick, united reaction from the rest of Europe. Indeed, he could not think it wise of Bonaparte to return at such a moment, while the diplomats remained in session and communication was easy. But perhaps the emperor understood human nature, and politics, better than most; his return could only be *un*wise if it were met with vigorous, united force—an end that could prove well beyond the proudly posturing parties in Vienna.

He had no clue when hostilities would open. But David knew he would be leaving soon. For the longer Bonaparte went unchallenged, the larger the army he would raise and retrain, and the greater the threat to all that had been gained over so many years of sacrifice.

After a visit to barracks, to check on any further news and to apply himself to an hour's worth of correspondence— ascertaining companions' plans and recalling his batman, Barton, from leave—David stopped in to see his brother at White's. Hayden's friends, the ubiquitous Lords Demarest and Knowles and the soon-to-be-wed George Gillen, were happily arranged about one of the club's card tables, on the verge of attacking their whist hands. But Hayden waved the others away as David approached.

"D'you know," Hayden said, leaning back in his seat as he carefully examined David's face, "last season held certain attractions. But this one is proving ticklish." He sighed. "I suppose they are all annoying in their fashion, though I do wish I'd departed for my tour last fall." He glanced down at his hand of cards. "When d'you go?"

David had to laugh. "You sound as though I am rather tediously contemplating an appointment with my tailor, Myles." At his brother's shrug he added, "I've been down to barracks. But my departure shall take some time to determine. Our forces in the Netherlands will of course be mobilized. And 'tis a foregone conclusion that Wellington must return from Vienna to oversee them. Word must have reached Vienna by now.

Other than that—" It was his turn to shrug. "What are you thinking?"

Again Hayden sighed. "Parliament will hope—as it should not—that Bonaparte will be content once again to head France. But there are objections to the man *per se.* We have had considerable opportunity to know Monsieur Bonaparte. Do *you* hold out any hope that he might be contained?"

"None at all."

"Nor do I. So there must be a vote once again for war. But once resolved that conflict is inevitable—a resolution, by the way, that could take some weeks—the Commons will dither when it should not. And there is that far-from-minor matter— that we must be ready to fight a war before we declare it. But I leave military matters to you and Wellington."

"I cannot imagine a decision before the Easter recess," David said, moving to take Demarest's vacated seat. "At least two weeks from now."

"At least," Hayden agreed with a smile. "Unless you hear from Wellington."

"He will not press me to join his staff again. He will find enthusiasm enough in younger officers. That has always carried weight with him. He might complain about inexperience, but he objects to long faces."

"And yours is a long face?"

"Increasingly. I am feeling old."

"But you still think you must go?"

"I must. It is an obligation. And a desire. If I am not there and feel that if I had been—"

"Ah! David Trent's exceptionality!"

" 'Tis hardly 'exceptionality,' Myles, when any confrontation is likely to turn on sheer numbers. We shall have difficulties enough in preparation without scrabbling for heads."

"The allies will come forward."

"Yes. And what a motley assortment we shall be!" His rest-

less fingers turned Demarest's cards for review before he
carefully repositioned the hand.

"How inscrutable you are," Hayden muttered, observing
him. "And what of your other obligation?"

"I have no other obligation. Miss Caswell has released me."

"Because of this news?"

David shook his head. "No. She threw me over last night.
Before any of us knew."

"Before . . . ?" Hayden repeated softly, watching his brother's
face. "Well, at least you might console yourself that she objects to you on your merits, or lack of them, and not because
of influences beyond your control."

"*You* might find consolation in such thinking, Hayden," he
objected quickly. "Though I doubt you have ever been refused."

"Not that I recall," Hayden admitted with a small smile.
"Though I've never offered, either."

" 'Tis not a pleasant feeling," David admitted with some
warmth. "The more so when she gave every indication . . ."
Catching Hayden's expression, he insisted instead, "She is not
indifferent to me. She tells me she has decided against me, but
my vanity tells me otherwise. I cannot believe her so fickle,
that in less than a fortnight in town she has turned her attentions to others." He firmed his lips, at once aware of sounding
too strident. The previous night's restless sleep still haunted
him; as a seasoned campaigner, he habitually slept like a top.
And the morning's requirements had fed his grievances.

Myles observed him with greater curiosity than amusement. " 'Tis simply the shock," he offered at last. "You will
come 'round."

"Oh, certainly. I've every faith in it! But it's a puzzle
nonetheless—that now the matter with Miss Caswell is
settled, I've an unexpected reluctance to have it so. I'd not realized, that when I contemplated selling up—and spending
time fishing and riding and eating as much buttered toast as I

might possibly want—that *she* was so essential a part of it. She has been one with my thoughts of home, Myles. Ever since the New Year."

"Well . . ." Hayden said. "News like today's certainly does concentrate the mind. But you had some years of fond attachment to make up in order to match her. As I recall, you claimed Miss Caswell would have to *choose* you. You gave her too much rein."

"The more fool I, though it was the honorable course. I should have taken your advice and deprived her of choice. D'you know," he diverted heatedly, "she believes me in thrall to Miss Athington?"

"Does she?" Hayden's eyebrows rose. "Astonishing. Where do women get these notions? But speakin' of notions—no doubt you've heard of Miss Caswell's apparent fondness for young Grenby. Some also suggest her interest grows in her brother's friend, Ronald Dumont."

At that David swore, low but volubly, in the French that always satisfied his more primitive feelings. That Billie should care in the slightest for the decorative, too smoothly mannered Grenby was outside of enough. And Dumont! What little David had seen of Dumont confirmed the man's venality. He was sly, calculating, and reliable as a swamp.

Hayden drummed his fingers upon the table felt. "Each time you cross the Channel, David, your *argot* becomes more colorful. I know your facility amuses *Grand-mère*, but *I* find it vulgar. If you will not engage in civilized conversation, I shall have at my cards."

David quickly apologized.

"I note you left the girl dangling more than two months," Hayden continued. "Even the most complacent of females would not have appreciated *that,* and Miss Caswell is far from complacent. She might well credit Miss Athington's aspirations, when she believes you insincere. You've just objected to Grenby and Dumont on much less provocation."

"She asked for the time. Whether we wed was always Miss Caswell's decision."

"Then perhaps she looks for more enthusiasm in you. She is too much like you, David, with too great a preference for action. She may interpret your reticence as indifference. Can you claim it isn't so? You have been too *nice.*"

David did not volunteer just how often he had been impertinent enough to steal kisses.

"She did say no?" Hayden pressed, watching his face with interest.

"Quite clearly. She says she does not want me—and that she might want others."

"No woman can be trusted to tell the truth."

"She is different."

"She is not." Hayden held up a palm as David would have protested. "Do you want my advice, or did you simply wish to squawk?"

"You do know how to flatter a man, Myles. God help you should you ever find yourself in like circumstances."

"I shan't," he countered. "And you must act as though your own position has not altered. You must act as though still betrothed. 'Twill be a kindness to both of you." Hayden must have read the disbelief on his face. "Oh, come, David. I know you can dissemble well enough to turn most Drury Lane thespians out on their ears. Haven't you convinced the world you're a good-hearted fellow?"

David ignored the jab. "Pretending nothing has changed hardly seems fair to her. I pressed her for a decision, and she gave me one."

Hayden shrugged. "*Mon frère,* you mustn't be disheartened. 'All is fair,'" he offered blandly, "'in love and war.' And you are at both. Besides"—he leaned back into his seat—"if you do not *act* engaged, you are apt to spend your meager time in town bein' pitied, like a proper fool. Best to keep the upper hand. Your strategy, Major, must be to fight for her."

"A tall order when, as you say, I may leave in a matter of days."

"The tactics must be your own." Hayden yawned. "Were I you, I shouldn't spend too much time reflecting on every pifflin' procedure."

" 'Piffling,' Myles? When did you ever?" As that elicited a smile, David added, "Your grand strategy forgets a potential snag. As Miss Caswell has probably already informed her father and brothers, they will enforce her will."

"Ah, yes, I'd forgotten the brothers. They are a proper team, aren't they?"

"And Kit in particular is a rackety fellow."

"Yes," Hayden mused aloud. "His vowels are no rarity. I've heard he's in deep with Dumont."

"Yet you tell me Dumont's name is linked to Billie Caswell's?"

"Perhaps for reasons other than affection. Sometimes snares are set for larger game."

David keenly felt his frustration. Kit Caswell appeared set to cause more distress for his family. He would end up in more than one black book. And once David himself was off on the Continent, he would have no means of aiding Billie.

"You are certain, Myles, about Kit Caswell?"

"These things are weighed at the tables, David. If Christopher Caswell does not make good on a great deal—and soon—things are likely to go ill for him."

"Surely *you* haven't tried him?"

Hayden smiled. "I'm not in the habit of fleecing puppies. And wagering with Caswell would be unseemly. Bein' all in the family."

"No longer."

"Nevertheless. Consider that I aid your subterfuge. But someone else will press him. And then I should worry about his sister—and her portion." David's dark thoughts must have been all too evident, for Hayden asked lightly, "What shall you be doing in the near term—as you see to the welfare of the realm?"

"I've curtailed Barton's leave and must help cajole those I might to rejoining. With luck there should be considerable *esprit*. And I must see *Grand-mère*."

As David rose to his feet, Hayden groaned. "She will take this badly," he said. "You are her favorite."

David's gaze measured him. "You are a fool, Myles."

Hayden shrugged. "Is there ought I might do to aid you?"

"You might keep an eye out for Kit Caswell and Dumont."

"Easy enough. Brothers are the very devil, aren't they?" And with Hayden's smile and idle salute, David found himself dismissed.

He mulled over Hayden's advice as he set about writing a letter to the Duke and Duchess of Braughton. He said nothing to his parents of Miss Caswell's defection, leaving that particular to Sir Moreton Caswell's communication. But David could not similarly mask from his grandmother the state of his heart or his plans to leave. When the dowager duchess received him that afternoon, she insisted that they go out at once to discuss matters on a drive in the park.

"*Grand-mère,* it is gray and chilly," he protested. "And you have been ill."

"*Non, mon brave.* We must have the air!" And so the stately barouche and four was ordered up, and David, tucking several lap robes about his octogenarian relative, watched her with concern.

"I do worry about your health, *Grand-mère*."

"Pah! You think me so decrepit? Perhaps you already have your eye on what I shall leave to you!"

David smiled broadly. "I assure you, I never think of such. I should have to wait a very long while in any event."

"Because *I* do not go to war." Her still strikingly attractive features were concerned as she squeezed his hand. "I worry for you, David."

"You know you mustn't. I have always returned to you."

She tried to smile. "This Bonaparte! I knew that he would do something like this!"

"Did you?" David laughed. "You cannot convince me that you suspected anything of the sort! If you did, you should have advised the rest of us. We might have been better prepared for his return."

She airily waved a tiny hand in an elegant glove. "He will believe himself welcome. He will believe himself *loved.* He has so much the swelled head! But it is only that King Louis has proved so weak."

"If no one dares counter him, Bonaparte will grasp power by default. He may not be loved, but he might still be effective."

"Perhaps he will be content to leave the rest of us alone."

"Do you think that likely, *Grand-mère*?"

She shook her head, crowned with its extravagantly beribboned bonnet. "I fear not. I fear not. But there is that chance— Ah!" she said waving. "There is Lady Eloise. Three times a widow! Does she not look spry?" *Grand-mère* was clearly delighted to be out, to see and to be seen, to tease her forbearing servants and her patient grandson. For some minutes she chattered about the others around them; then she asked abruptly, "And now, *mon petit*, what of your *affaire de coeur*?"

"*Affaire de coeur, Grand-mère*? There is no love affair. Miss Caswell has dismissed me."

He supposed it encouraging that she should look so surprised.

"You have lost her?"

"I am not certain, *Grand-mère*," he said dryly, "that she was mine to lose. Did you not tell me at the New Year that her 'puppy love' would pass?"

"That might have been replaced by something deeper."

"Apparently not."

"Ah! You are *brusque* with me! So she broke with you just this morning—with this news?"

"No. Before. Yesterday evening."

"Before . . ." she said softly, in much the same considering tone of voice Hayden had used. "Then perhaps she now regrets—and will change her mind."

"If so, she must be patient. I do not intend to see her again for some time."

"But that is cruel, David! Your Miss Billie will wish to see you. You are not one to play at the games." At which David dared not divulge his intention to follow Hayden's strategy and play very much "at the games."

"While I am away, *Grand-mère,*" he said, diverting her, "I should appreciate it if you would look to Miss Caswell's interests. If she is truly captivated by those suitors mentioned here in town, I must doubt her judgment. She is very young and has been left too much to her own devices."

"Perhaps she is tired of being treated as so young. She is what—eighteen?"

"Nineteen. But I fear her parents—preoccupied as they were by Lady Caswell's ill health—were always most inattentive. And one brother, Kit, is nothing but trouble."

"Children suffer from improper attention—from indulgence—as well as the neglect," she intoned sagely.

"And what were our failings, then, *Grand-mère?*" he teased her.

"My grandsons do not fail. I took great care it should not be so." She smiled. "*Mais, il reste à savoir!* It remains to be seen!"

As he laughed, she watched him fondly for a moment before turning to look out at the park.

"I remember *la gamine* Billie," she said, "from many years ago."

"You knew that 'Billie' Caswell was a girl?"

She glanced quickly and reprovingly across at him. "But of course!" Her attention returned to the activity of parading vehicles around them. "Such early spirit can become too bold," she mused aloud, "rude and rough. What in a child is mere *frolic* grows to the wildness of the hoyden, to much that is forward, immodest, and ill-mannered—"

"She is none of these," David interrupted. "You know she is not."

His *grand-mère* turned again to him with a raised eyebrow. "Yes, I know that she is not. Miss Billie Caswell is now a lovely lady, who has most pleasing manners and plays the piano *comme un ange*—if Hayden is to be believed."

"Hayden told you of her playing?"

"You think your brother hasn't the ear?"

"I did not think he troubled to observe."

"Your brother always observes," she said wryly. "He very seldom *acts*. But I believe he may have some interest in Miss Billie."

"Hayden?"

Grand-mère pursed her lips as she stared repressively at him. "Take care, my so blind David, that you do not lose your precious Billie. Do you not hear yourself? You are the tinderbox! Monsieur Bonaparte interferes, yes. It is very bad of him. But you must not let him interfere in all! You have not given this the thought you should—and yet you have had months. You have let resentment rule your heart. No wonder that Miss Billie sends you away and entertains pretty Lord Grenby, when you make so obvious the surly sacrifice!"

As he still clasped one of his grandmother's hands, he gently rubbed his thumb across the back of her soft glove. "I see I should have been wiser," he said at last. " 'Tis why I shall never be a general. I do not think of all that I should."

"You may yet be a general, *mon brave,* though I believe you think *too* much for it!" She smiled. "No, David, if anything shall stop you, it will be that you are too kind."

"You will regret saying that some day, *Grand-mère*." He laughed, leaning to kiss her thin cheek. "When you wish to tease me."

"I shall not regret. Where one loves, one does not regret. But yes! You must give me many more chances to tease you!" And for the remainder of their drive, as they spoke in the French that was her preference, her high spirits and enthusiasm for the gayest of company kept her happily engaged with those they encountered—and focused on less troubling matters.

Chapter Eight

The anxiety in town that weekend lacked precedent. Despite Parliament's vote on Friday to impose the widely unpopular Corn Laws, despite the end of the hubbub and protests associated with that issue, no relief was in sight, for the news of Bonaparte's escape and advance toward Paris swamped all else.

Billie had been too young to recall the nation's fear of France at the turn of the century, when an invasion across the Channel seemed imminent. She had nothing to which to compare the current preparations for war. But such preparations now appeared all-encompassing. In church that Sunday the congregation was exhorted to hold fast and true in the trying times ahead—all the best of advice, Billie was certain, but she could only dwell on the fact that David Trent did not return to her.

She had delayed writing to her father, convinced as she was that there was no real harm in ignoring her broken engagement. Since there had been no public announcement of intentions, she reasoned that no assurance of a subsequent break needed to be made. Such an argument seemed entirely logical, at least as an excuse for not rushing to put pen to paper. And her father, in any event, would be most concerned about Kit.

With the first news, her brother had been wild with excitement, threatening to join up at once. But his situation was such that he had no funds to purchase colors. From what Billie had heard, he owed money to half the *ton*. And their father would never consent to an additional investment. For the first time Billie felt grateful that Kit was so thoroughly beholden to his creditors—if it kept him away from the Continent and from danger.

The world moved with breathtaking speed. All thought of an idle, frivolous season had been set aside to prepare for confrontation. There was yet more to be endured, in as cool and composed a manner as possible. Yet it was difficult, as Billie discovered, to feel entirely cool and composed when one's brother strolled into the drawing room in the newly issued uniform of an infantry officer.

"Kit! What have you done?"

"Rather obvious, wouldn't you say, Billie?" He was beaming with pride and exhilaration. "I've purchased a commission—as a lowly lieutenant, to be sure. But I'm an officer, nonetheless, in the Fifty-second. Alan Athington's regiment."

"Are you mad, Kit? How can you afford such a thing?"

"Why, I thought you'd be pleased for me!" And Billie found his astonishment almost as provoking as his ill-considered action. "Old Trahearne made it possible—by making me the loan. He's all for battling Bonaparte. I know I ought to pay off the IOUs to Dumont, but there's time enough for that later. Dumont will continue to stake me. He is the best friend in the world."

"*Friend!*" Billie barely kept her voice level. "A 'friend' would never have encouraged you to play so deep to begin with. And the truest of gentlemen would have folded a good hand rather than press you. I know *that* much, Kit. Mr. Dumont imposes upon you—upon us—for some purpose of his own. He's been associated with much that's unpleasant, and . . . and I understand his family is most disappointed in him. And now you put your *life* at risk!"

Kit's features had set stubbornly. "I don't see why you should be so hard on Dumont. Even if he's out a bit of blunt at the moment, he knows I've wanted to join up. None of the family could see it," he charged. "All of you have chosen to ignore my wishes—as usual."

"For your own good, Kit. You've chosen one foolish course after another—"

"Only because I wasn't let to do what I wanted! You know that, Billie. I thought you understood." As she worried her lower lip, he added, "And Dumont isn't the loathsome fellow you make him. He tells me how much he esteems you."

" 'Esteems' me? He 'esteems' my portion!"

"Well"—Kit dared smile—"it is something to consider, isn't it? Do not fool yourself that your smart Major Trent hasn't thought of it!"

"I think I can safely claim that he hasn't! It would never signify. Lord David may not have what his brother, Hayden, has, but he will most certainly be well set up."

"Then why did he ever take to soldiering?"

"I—I haven't a clue. Perhaps, like you, he prefers to strut about in scarlet! Oh, I think you are all mad!" That she should then, inexplicably, choose to cry startled both of them.

"Such stuff, Billie!" Kit scoffed, wrinkling his nose at her, as though he were still thirteen. "If anything, I'd have thought you'd want to come with me!"

"Perhaps I do," she asserted, raising her chin and refusing to dab at her damp eyes. "But I know that I cannot. I must stay with Aunt Ephie and Morty, who will stick to Miss Urquhart. My days of adventure are past now, Kit."

His light brown eyes, so like her own, examined her minutely. "You and Ephie might locate to Brussels for the season. Many families plan to follow the troops. Athington's said his company will probably be off to Ostend within days. And Miss Athington and her parents will follow him to Brussels."

"Will they?" Billie echoed faintly. "She did not tell me."

"Oh, half the *ton* will be in Brussels. 'Twill be the liveliest place in the world. And what sport—to see Boney take his lickings!"

Such ill-reasoned ardor only further incensed her.

"You do not know what you are about," she managed steadily. "I am surprised that your colonel—that they would even think of sending someone so green! But it's too late for me—or for Father—to stop you, and so I must wish you well. You must try to—try to *think,* Kit! Oh, was I ever as headstrong as you are? No wonder he believes me—"

When she stopped, Kit's look was puzzled, but he smiled at her continued silence. "You know I love you, Billie," he claimed easily.

"Do you?" She sighed. "I suspect 'tis rather that you know I love *you*—and you play upon it. You've been indulged, Kit, and I fear it will not serve you well."

"Whatever!" he pronounced, proudly raising his chin. "I'm happy now. If you must fret, fret over whom you might choose to marry—now that Trent will be leaving. If you will not have Dumont, the bets are on Grenby, or Willard Trahearne."

"The bets? I cannot find such attention flattering. And Mr. Trahearne is a decade older than Papa, Kit. Would you truly have me consider such a man?"

"I've seen his property at Fairways. I can well imagine you mistress of such a place, Billie. And Grenby isn't bad either— though one can't help wishing to scuff him up a bit."

She smiled. Lord Grenby was indeed always turned out as neatly as a new penny.

"I'm just pleased Trent will be well out of the running," Kit continued. "Almost anyone but David Trent might do."

"Why, Kit?" she asked frankly. "Why have you always disliked him so?"

"Maybe because you've always *liked* him so—for no reason I could ever discover. He always had at *you* worse than any of the rest of us."

"I plagued him. And he thought me a boy. I certainly acted like one."

"Well, then, he's blind as well as dim-witted, and I shall be glad never to see him again."

"Don't—don't say so, Kit. Not now. Not when there is so much at stake."

Kit shrugged. "What is he to me anyway? I shan't give him another thought. Now kiss me, Billie, for I won't be back to see you for at least another two weeks."

She gave him a swift peck on the cheek and saw him on his way, then searched out her aunt, to convey Kit's news. Ephie thankfully refrained from much comment, but only because they were due to attend the Birdwistles' ball that night, and they had little time to ready themselves.

The evening's event proved remarkable for its fierce dedication to pleasure. Though a scarcely acknowledged thread of tension ran through the company, Billie counted no trembling lips or tearful glances among the elegant guests at Twyla Birdwistle's come out. And though Billie too readily recalled her Shakespeare, and the forebodings associated with the ides of March, she willfully smothered any agitation—and failed to spot it in others.

As she and Ephie were announced and made their way into the gaily decorated ballroom, one of the largest and most beautifully adorned rooms in town, Billie soon attracted the attentions of eager Lord Grenby and several other faithful swains. But Lord David was not to be spotted amid the crowd of uniformed officers taking time to attend the ball.

She had not seen him in six momentous days. Indeed, as she attempted to share in the lighthearted banter about her, she kept one expectant eye upon the door.

"Do you watch for Lord David?" Charis asked her, so cheerfully that Billie dearly wished she might smite her. "I hear he has already left for Dover," her tormentor continued callously. "I had it from my brother Alan on Monday."

"I was not watching for him," Billie lied, "but for Lord Grenby's return with my punch."

Charis' grin was close to a smirk. "Perhaps you have not heard, Miss Caswell, that I shall be moving with my family to Brussels for the spring."

"I had heard, Miss Athington. Where shall you stay?"

"Papa has leased a house just one block from the Place Royale. We shall be able to see the troops parade from our front parlor!"

"How happy for you. You are not concerned about your brother—and the coming confrontation?"

"Oh, Alan assures us that it will probably come to naught. We must be ready, but Bonaparte will never regain his former support. And even if he does, why should he attack the allies?" She laughed. "You mustn't look so serious, Miss Billie."

"I still think it might be wise of you, Miss Athington, to consider—when you pack your trunks—that you might at some point need to evacuate."

"To evacuate? How droll! It shan't prove at all dangerous. Why, much of London society shall be taking up residence in Brussels. Easily half the city shall be English, as Papa has it."

"One might then feel quite at home when under siege, I suppose," Billie said.

Charis laughed. "You are most amusing, Miss Billie."

"I don't mean to be. Perhaps I play Cassandra this evening and warn you that Bonaparte has always moved with secrecy and swiftness. Witness his recent escape from Elba."

"Well said, Miss Caswell," Lord Grenby remarked, coming up to hand her a glass of lemonade. "We mustn't be too confident." But Grenby's wide and self-consciously attractive smile was supremely confident.

Charis Athington's gaze narrowed upon them. "You both might consider joining the society in Brussels," she proposed. "London is likely to be left very dull."

"I am finding entertainment enough here, Miss Athington," Grenby assured her, with a gracious bow to Billie.

Billie felt the color rise to her cheeks. She had not intended to encourage Grenby so particularly, yet he appeared to be most particularly encouraged. In distraction she looked to the sea of regimental scarlet across the room. *He has gone,* she thought. *He has already gone to Dover and is probably even now crossing to Brussels.* She felt the notion almost as a physical pain. But her unhappy gaze soon focused on the distinctive brass buttons in front of her—on the familiar paired facings of a Coldstream officer's tunic.

"Oh!" she breathed, as her gaze rose to meet Lord David's. "You are still here."

"I hope you do not object, Miss Wilhelmina," he said lightly. His eyes looked very bright.

She thought her discomposure something in the nature of an illness, that she should always delight so mindlessly in merely looking at him.

"Have you this dance for me?" he persisted, looking to Grenby.

The man obligingly opened his palm to Billie. "It is Miss Caswell's to confer," he allowed, though he did not look pleased when Billie chose to give the major her hand.

As they walked onto the floor, David inclined his head to hers. "Your Lord Grenby looks disappointed this evening," he whispered, stepping away to take his place in the set. "Have you not told him I am yesterday's suitor?"

As the music began, Billie did not answer him. There seemed so much to say; she did not wish to waste a minute discussing Lord Grenby. Yet it did occur to her that in his manner of claiming a dance, and in calling her Miss Wilhelmina, the major had not acted in the least like "yesterday's suitor."

He was smiling at her now in a way that would convince no one of a lapsed attachment.

"I heard you were in Dover," she said.

"Very briefly. We must move thousands. As quickly as possible."

"But we do not yet know what Bonaparte will do!"

"Don't we?"

She lost him in the figures of the dance. When they came back around together once more, she found the brief clasp of his hand heartening.

"What do you expect?" she asked tensely.

He smiled. "This is much too grim a conversation—for a ball."

"I am no simpleton, Major, to be fed assurances."

With one raised eyebrow, he affirmed, "No." And when they met again, he told her, "Parliament will take its time debating war, while the army prepares to wage it. And we will watch Bonaparte."

When she again had his ear, she protested, "All this was settled last year!"

"This summer will truly resolve it."

"But surely none of it is necessary! He must be content with France. We needn't be involved—"

When he returned, he said, "You anticipate the debate, Miss Billie. 'Tis a debate I shan't be staying to hear."

She thought rather desperately, *When? When must you leave?* But instead she chose to relay that Kit had obtained a commission.

The major looked very serious for a moment. "I suppose such was to be expected. Your brother is an impulsive fellow."

"Would you deny"—she charged, instantly taking umbrage—"that more men are needed?"

"Certainly not. But trained men. Steady men. Calm and levelheaded soldiers. I don't wish to presuppose—"

"But you do!" As one eyebrow again rose at that, and not in amusement, she added, "Oh, I do not know why I defend him— when I do not wish him to go!"

"But you wish me to go?"

She looked at him then without commenting, wondering why he could not see. She had never thought herself so fine an actress. As the dance moved into a more rapid reel, they could no longer speak at all. Billie felt the frustration of fading, precious time. Though she had thought to be elated in his presence once more, the ball had become a misery.

When the set ended, he did not surrender her but drew her quickly to the long, columned hall at the side of the ballroom. Other couples passed in and out of the many curtained openings; she and the major were in full view of most at the dance. Yet their removal to the hall gave them a limited privacy and quiet that Billie welcomed.

"Now," he said, leaning close to her. His gaze was very steady. "You might talk."

When Billie's attention slipped to the side to locate Ephie a good twenty yards across the room, the major noted her concern.

"We are most properly positioned," he assured her softly.

But you take the same liberties, she thought, *as though we were still betrothed.* Her chin rose.

"You know that Miss Athington removes to Brussels with her family?" she asked.

"She has told me."

"I imagine that will be most convenient," she suggested.

"For whom? Wellington—or Bonaparte?"

She stifled a laugh and forced herself to concentrate on his smoothly-shaven chin. "You . . . you mustn't make me laugh."

"It pleases me to do so," he said with a smile. "'Tis often for the best. And you are much too serious this evening."

"There are serious events at hand."

"You think you must remind me?" Again his smile caught her attention. "Do you contemplate following the Athingtons and the rest of the throng to Brussels?"

"No. Father would not permit me to leave, even if Morty could be prevailed upon. Though I do worry for Kit. . . ."

"He must take his lumps."

"You've expressed that view before, Major," she said quickly.

"Yes. I am staunch as a post." This time his smile did not convey humor. "I do not wish to cross you, Miss Billie. I imagine there is nothing more calculated to raise your ire. And I would not presume to patronize, to advise your father—or your brother Morty—against it. But you must not go to Brussels. This is not a play staged for society's amusement. There are real risks—"

"Major," she interrupted proudly, "I have just been warning Miss Athington very much as you warn me now."

"Is that so? Wise Miss Billie!" He surveyed her features indulgently. "'Tis far better for you to have your season," he mused aloud, "away from Leicestershire and your cares."

"And now you *do* patronize, Major!" When she would have stepped back from him, she ran up against the velvet drapes at one column's edge. "You would have me cosseted here, with vacated theaters and drawing rooms, while you and the rest of the kingdom romp in Brussels."

"I foresee little time to 'romp' in Brussels," he countered smoothly. Then he added—and not entirely to the point—"The Household regiments locate west of town. At Enghien. More than twenty miles away. And do not"—he playfully tapped her chin with one finger—"go blurting that to the French."

"Oh . . ." She tried to hide her satisfaction. In her estimation he could not be too far removed from Brussels.

"Are you possibly jealous, Miss Billie?" he persisted, an amused sparkle in his gaze.

"Of your ability to *act,* to *do* something, yes," she admitted, refusing to gratify him, and keeping her thoughts of Charis Athington to herself.

"You think you would like to follow the drum?" he asked, shaking his head. "With your youth and energy you would chafe at its plodding beat. You'd find it only wearing, and the life would age you ten years in one." His look now was solemn.

"I cannot speak to you as though you were a man. For the life of me, I cannot think of you so. But as you say, you are no simpleton. And I must be honest. Take your season as it's offered, and try to be content."

"While you have your war."

" 'Tis not my war. You are unkind."

"But you have called me brave," she asserted.

"No empty words." Again he smiled. " 'Tis true. But it takes equal courage, Miss Billie, probably greater courage, to be patient while confronting the imagined demons—those of worry, and anxiety, and regret. I have seen men go mad with waiting. And waiting—sheer, numbing tedium—is nine-tenths of service."

"Which is why you need Bonaparte—as an excuse for a battle."

"He is not an excuse," he countered grimly. "He is a reason."

"You *want* the reason."

"No, I am *persuaded* by the reason." The comment was sharp. "I would never have believed you could sound so . . . *missish!*"

At once she was conscious of the color in her cheeks, of the stares and hushed attention about them. No one had approached them; they had been left to themselves. But Ephie, her gaze very stern, had come closer. And Billie knew their quarrel was a subject of speculation.

"We—we take too much time," she said. She found she could not move either to the right or the left of him without brushing against him. She met his gaze, prepared to ask him to kindly step aside, only to encounter a considering look in his that she could not quite interpret.

"Every once in a while," he said, "the reminder strikes me like a blow."

"What reminder, Major?" She tried to turn into the column, to squeeze past his broad chest, but there was no room.

"The reminder that you are indeed a very young miss." And

with that extraordinary admission, he smoothly slipped his arm about her waist. Drawing her from their singularly exposed spot, he pulled her into the set for the waltz.

"You mustn't—you mustn't dance another with me," she said, conscious of the firmness in his clasp.

"No?" He surveyed the dance floor instead of looking at her. "We shan't avoid the alert eyes and ears of *The Tattler* in any event. At least I choose to be understood."

"But this is our third dance!"

"Just so." He smiled broadly at her. "If a simple tiff must be bruited about, at least *The Tattler* might acknowledge the reason for it."

"We are not engaged," Billie insisted, forced to follow him in the dance. She knew he mustn't claim again what she'd attempted to sever. She gathered the will to break from him at the first opportunity—their "tiff" might entail so much. But catching sight of Charis Athington's envious expression as they passed, Billie found she preferred one victory to another.

"The world will not be ignored just now, Miss Billie," the major remarked idly as they stepped on down the set. "It is 'too much with us,' as the poet says. On all sides, apparently." His hold tightened. "Do smile, sweet. I cannot act happy for both of us."

"I am not happy."

"Ah, I forget. You are upset that I shall be leaving you. Very good. You think ahead of me."

No, she thought, *I do not think ahead of you. 'Twould be quite impossible to think ahead of you*. She looked directly at him.

"You may be an actor," she said. "But I am not."

"So you do not wish me to go?" His gaze held hers. "I believe I asked earlier—before our refreshing little break."

"If I—if I were to ask you to stay, would you?"

His hold about her waist felt strong as a vise.

"You would not ask me," he claimed, suddenly serious.

"Which is why you make it so devilishly difficult to leave."
He turned their clasped hands unexpectedly to his lips and
quickly kissed her wrist below her glove.

She thought he could not go then, not after such outrageous
behavior. She silently studied his face for the remainder of the
dance, anticipating that they must have further conversation.
But he did go, with no more than a farewell at the waltz's end
and just after returning her to a disapproving Ephie.

The next morning Billie received a small volume of Words-
worth's poetry, accompanied by a typically terse note from
the major, explaining that it had been among some books
from Braughton that he had gathered to take with him. He
wrote: *I hope you will consider this a gift. It is, like my heart,
now yours.* Sous bonne garde. *David.*

Chapter Nine

She was left to find Enghien in the atlas—and to spend too much time puzzling over David Trent's parting note. Again she concluded that he meant to be cryptic. Given his hasty, dashed phrases and lack of punctuation, he left one to infer too much. *Sous bonne garde.* Did that mean he knew his heart to be safe in her keeping? Or that she must not worry about him—that he was in the safekeeping of others? In the care of the Duke of Wellington, perhaps, or of even higher authority? She hoped all military communications did not suffer so from lack of clarity.

Apprehension filled her days. Shortly after Lord David's departure, word arrived from Vienna that the Congress of allies had declared Napoléon Bonaparte an "enemy of the world." Bonaparte reached Paris on the same day that Louis XVIII, the installed Bourbon king, fled the city. Given the astonishing speed of Bonaparte's advance and the overwhelming welcome his countrymen had given him, a confrontation between France and the rest of Europe seemed inevitable. Still, Bonaparte claimed to want only peace with his neighbors, though no one with whom Billie spoke believed as much.

Over the Easter break, during the last week in March, even Billie's brother Edward spoke of possibly curtailing his studies to join up and fight Bonaparte. With some effort Billie, Ephie, and Morty convinced him that he should first finish reading for his degree—that Bonaparte might still be there for him some months later.

By the time the Commons did begin debate on the matter of war, in late April, many forces—including Alan Athington's company of the 52nd—had already made their way across the Channel to join the remnants of the allied army in Brussels. Wellington, who had arrived in Brussels the first week in April, was heard to claim that the clash—if it came—would not occur before July. In an effort to amass as large and overwhelming a force for him as possible, Britain and Ireland were even stripped of their garrisons. All the more reason, then, for Kit Caswell to chafe at the fact that his own company was directed to stay at home. Kit's disappointment in that, coupled with the exceeding boredom of constant drilling in preparation for a conflict he apparently was destined to miss, had him impatiently reverting to previous form. Once again he took to excessive gaming in the company of Ronald Dumont and P.B. Marsh.

Appalled by Kit's increasing debts, Billie implored him to limit his wagers—to no avail. A letter of appeal to their father, Sir Moreton, only elicited the advice to let Kit learn his lesson and "reward himself for his own folly"; Sir Moreton appeared to believe that the Marshes and Dumonts of the world could do no lasting harm. Billie suspected otherwise, her resentment of the gentlemen's influence over her brother grew, and whenever she did encounter Ronald Dumont, she made a point of "cutting" him, which annoyed Kit more than it did Dumont.

"Can't you like Dumont—even a little?" Kit coaxed her after a particularly public snub.

"I cannot," Billie assured him, and she returned to contemplating that morning's *Times*. She had consistently, and with no small amount of pain, refused to lend as much as a shilling to Kit while he kept company with Ronald Dumont. She took seriously Kit's repeated threats to "get on with the business" and flee to the Continent, because she knew Kit very well and knew that his impatience mirrored her own.

Morty and his adoring Esther Urquhart announced their engagement, which afforded Billie some relief from considering her own uncertain status. London's gossip pages in *The Tattler* never did trouble to carry an item concerning Miss Caswell and Lord David. Still, though she retained partners enough, none of Billie's admirers was as ardent as before. Major Trent's manifest "claim" at the Birdwistle ball had put them off. Only elderly Mr. Trahearne persisted, with a halfhearted gallantry Billie ascribed more to habit, or to forgetfulness, than to any sincere interest. Elegant Lord Grenby turned his attentions to May Sanders, a substitution that made little sense to Billie—until Hayden, who had escorted Billie and her aunt on a first foray to Almack's, advised her that the Sanders' fortune would keep Grenby in acceptable style for some years.

"And they shall suit," he remarked as his gaze followed hers, watching the couple dance. "Grenby is not a bad fellow, but there is not much to 'im."

"Unlike your brother."

"Do you doubt it, Miss Caswell?"

Billie's chin rose. Her brothers had trained her in meeting a challenge.

"Why was Lord David sent down from Oxford?"

"What?" Hayden's smile was broad. "Has he not told you?"

"I . . . have not asked him."

"Then it can't have seemed important," he concluded.

"But all those years of study wasted!"

"Oh, nothing of the sort! They weren't wasted, I assure you. David has a fine, shaggy head full of knowledge. Attendance is the thing, after all. I scarcely managed two years at the place m'self." When next Hayden caught her accusing eye, he added, "If the matter troubles you, Miss Billie, you must ask him—when he returns," he suggested with an easy confidence she was far from sharing.

Hayden had sought her company frequently enough during the spring that Billie suspected him of keeping her under some form of surveillance. She might have objected to his polite attentions, if she had not overheard Dumont once accuse Hayden of "spoiling the play" with Kit. Concluding that the Trents' sense of responsibility extended not only to herself but to keeping Kit from disaster, Billie was too sensible to desire an end to Hayden's company. And though Morty commented with some irritation that Hayden seemed to pop up everywhere, he also acknowledged the accompanying, increased *éclat* in the eyes of the *ton*.

Worry was Billie's most constant companion. She followed the news and the debates in Commons with something approaching dread. The weather did not help. An unusually cloudy, wet spring was apparently visited upon all of Europe. One did not venture out without vexations of one sort or another—damp hemlines, soggy shoes, delays, and drooping spirits. Though society was not as dull as Charis Athington had forecast—there were certainly bodies enough attending every event of note—no one appeared very gay. Billie knew she was dispirited, moving halfheartedly through the steps of her own season. She wished she might be off to Brussels herself, or quietly at home, rather than living in a state of feigned pleasure and constant suspension. Merely enduring the days, though they were nothing if not comfortable, required an application of will. That anyone else around her could even appear blithely unconcerned drew her disbelief.

Billie sought activity and motion, though the rain limited her choices. As Ephie did not keep horses, the offers of carriage rides from her "suitors" were usually, and gratefully, accepted. Billie took one or both of Ephie's footmen and walked miles, as none of the maids could match her pace. And she practiced the piano until her shoulders and arms ached. The

Dowager Duchess of Braughton, David's *grand-mère,* asked Billie over to play for her, and Billie enjoyed the visits. The duchess was enthusiastic and kind. But several sessions were enough, as the visits reminded her too distressingly of the absent Lord David, whom the duchess now never failed to mention. Billie suspected that the older woman *knew.* Yet Billie did not understand herself. Surely, surely she should have preferred any company associated with *him,* though *he* was not of the company?

The next time the duchess invited Billie over to play, Billie pleaded a headache.

As the month of May bore on, as the debates in Parliament resolved themselves into a declaration, by both houses, for war, and as word filtered from France that Bonaparte had managed to remobilize and retrain hundreds of thousands of soldiers, Billie's agitation found no suitable outlet.

May Sanders approached her at an afternoon's call and breathlessly relayed that she had had several letters at once from Charis Athington.

"She had set them aside and forgotten to post them—can you imagine? They are all on alert for Bonaparte. Charis says there is some talk of removing with her family to Antwerp for safety. But nothing untoward has happened *yet,* though she does say that they see the troops assembled nearly every day and that the Duke of Wellington lives just one block away from them and that he is to be encountered simply *everywhere.* Charis' brother—you did meet Alan, did you not, Miss Caswell?— brings his fellow officers by the house often, and Charis has met many others from all the armies, including the handsome and most gallant Dutch Prince of Orange. If Charis is to be believed, he has paid her some marked attention! I suppose, in all fairness, one must allow that Charis *is* lovely! Am I not a very good friend to say so? Oh—and she has seen Major Trent."

Billie fixed May with a determinedly cool gaze.

"Has she?"

"Oh, yes! And she said that he looked very well but that by the time he arrived at the dance at—at the Royal Palace, I believe—her card was already full. But he spent some time speaking with her brother, and the Household regiments are at Egg . . . Egg . . ."

"Enghien."

"What? Oh, yes. Enghien. How funny that sounds! And the major said that the duke expects three days' notice of any move by Bonaparte, so Charis thinks they might all safely remove from Brussels."

"Who intends to remove from Brussels, Miss Sanders?"

"Why, the Athingtons, of course."

Billie, still trying to make sense of May's scrambled talk, refused to dwell on how full Charis' dance card had been. Although that did not necessarily mean that David had even asked her. . . .

"Miss Caswell, did you hear me? I said that Charis said they had invited Major Lord David to dine. And he promised to attend them at the first opportunity. So you must see that he is well looked after, is he not?" And May, batting her falsely friendly, wide blue eyes, held Billie's steady gaze.

"I am sure the major—or any soldier—must be glad of fine food and pleasant company on occasion."

"Oh, as to that, they are all living exceptionally well, if Charis reports correctly. One would think it a regular holiday—and the place not filled with half the alarm we've had here at home! To hear her tell it, all is lively bustle and excitement! How I do wish Papa had taken me over as well! Only then I should not have had the company of dear Grenby . . ." As May's blue gaze once again settled in seeming innocence upon her, Billie determined that she had had enough and excused herself.

Lively bustle and excitement! Living exceptionally well! Promising to dine with Charis! And all this while *she* had been losing sleep! In a decidedly aggrieved mood, Billie returned

home, telling Ephie during the carriage ride back only that May
Sanders had once again had too much to say for herself.

The evening post had brought a letter in David Trent's distinctive hand. Under Ephie's close scrutiny, Billie shed her
pelisse and settled by the hearthside to read the missive that
had taken nearly a week to reach her.

Brussels, 25 May

Dear Miss Caswell,

*I hope you will pardon my long silence. I have found
few pauses for reflection, given the pressing needs to as-
semble, house, feed, and otherwise supply many men in a
short period of time, much less train soldiers who have
not been under arms for the better part of a year—if ever.*

*Only in these past two days have I returned to Brussels
for my first visit since arriving in the Low Countries at the
end of March. At that time, viewed from the canal boat from
Ostend, the peaceful countryside would never have been
described as anticipating war. All was greening pasture,
sleeping waterways, promisingly pollarded trees, and hum-
ble farms. Given the addition of so many tens of thousands
of troops since, that atmosphere has altered considerably.*

*I have quarters with a farming family just outside the
town I mentioned. They have been generous, and the lady
of the house is an excellent cook. But I dare not suppose
their support. The countryside is riddled with spies and
sympathizers with Bonaparte, as many of the men fought
for the emperor's armies in past years. I dare not be more
explicit. I ride out daily on the back roads, where the in-
habitants are not as discreet as they might be—I regret
that our allied soldiers are no more so—with regard to
what they observe of Bonaparte's movements. The local
farmers tend to forget that some of us have a passing
knowledge of the language. But few are openly hostile; if*

we should prove victorious this summer, the locals will of course claim to have prayed for us all along.

I had the opportunity shortly after arrival of touring the Belgian border with the Duke of Wellington's party, riding from Ostend at the Channel through Ypres and Ghent and farther south, in an effort to ascertain the state of allied defenses. The duke, I assure you, knows his ground and the challenges before him; we have, as we have always had, every confidence in his leadership. He is an extraordinary commander.

We continue to augment infantry, but, per the above, most of the Belgian troops cannot be relied upon. There is also much resentment among these French-speaking troops of last year's treaty granting control over Belgium to the Netherlands. Wellington is wisely mingling our many allied nationalities in all divisions and weaving among them differing levels of experience as well. There is insurance in this, though I must allow that the frustrations are perhaps equal to the benefits.

Despite this preparation I continue to hope, from what I hear from London, that war might be avoided. Perhaps a similar hope delays Parliament, which has yet to settle upon a "stance." Word is out that Bonaparte has political problems at home in France. Rumor claims he might be toppled there before he can pounce elsewhere. As we are in no state yet to take the battle to him, we must bide our time and observe.

Yet I cannot describe to you the unease here in Brussels. Whatever the political developments, hostilities must be anticipated. All must prepare for them, though we make every effort to do so with least alarm. Given the circumstances, I might have wished the British population in the city smaller and less excitable. One distinctly feels part of the season's entertainments. But the duke, bless him, seems to find the society congenial.

At camp we are content and comfortable, though I be-lieve it has rained every day now for almost two months; there is little to distinguish any of us in our constant state of drenched dampness. I understand I share some of your clouds, if not the delight of your company. My grand-mère *writes that she has had that particular plea-sure. I am happy to hear it; I confess, I am exceedingly fond of her. I thank you for your kindness in indulging her.*

From what I have ascertained, I believe your brother's company detailed at home, which is no doubt an unal-loyed disappointment for him but should be of consider-able comfort to you.

Do you remember our friend, Miss Athington? I have just had the opportunity to renew the acquaintance at a dance given by the Prince of Orange. Miss Athington in-quired as to your health; I could not assure her of it. I would ask how you do, Miss Caswell, if I did not fear the inquiry would impose upon you too great a burden of re-sponse.

Indeed, I hope you will not be offended by this commu-nication from me. However presumptuous, I claim the right based on the circumstances under which we parted, which were—to my mind—entirely amicable. I have no wish to prove a nuisance. I know that by now you must have written your father regarding the state of your heart, though in all these weeks I have heard naught of the matter from mine. But surely, whatever the case, Sir Moreton will understand that such a course never did run smooth.

Please forgive this letter's length. I am not usually long-winded, but I find I miss your company. Believe me sincere in wishing you well and happy.

Yours,
David

She could hardly complain that this letter was "cryptic"; she could hardly complain that it was terse. But in giving her less over which she might puzzle, he had also given her imagination less room. Were his sentiments still as strong as he had earlier implied? Despite the warmth of its tone, the missive struck her as merely genial and somehow reserved—as though he were just there amid a roomful of callers and speaking not to her alone.

"Is it bad news?" Ephie asked sharply. And Billie was at once conscious of holding the letter limply open upon her lap.

"No—no, not at all."

"You were frowning."

Billie forced a smile. "He tells me of the unease in Brussels. There is little new in that."

Ephie's gaze was too discerning. "It looks a longish letter," she said, "simply to speak of 'unease.'"

"He writes also of the preparations for war. And that he has just seen Miss Athington in Brussels."

"Indeed?" Again Ephie's gaze was too bright. "She always appeared to have quite a preference for the major's company."

Billie gratefully turned her attention to the tea that had just been brought to them. She would reread the letter later. There had been something encouraging, perhaps, in his comment that "such a course never did run smooth." The allusion, as she remembered it, was to Shakespeare, and the course of *true love* never running smooth.

"I never do take milk in my tea, Billie dear," Ephie reminded her.

"Yes, I am so sorry, Auntie." As she poured another cup, feeling her heightened color, she could hear Monty's angry voice in the hall. When her brother joined them in the parlor, he looked furious.

"Kit has run off," he snapped. "Borrowed more funds from a moneylender. A *moneylender,* Billie! And without leave from his regiment he maneuvered a spot as an army aide in

Brussels. How they shall employ the bedlamite, I haven't a clue! Probably have him polish the general's boots! Well, he was wild for going over and action. Now he has what he wanted! Might even be there by now. No one's seen him for two days. But *I* shall have to explain it to Father!"

Billie could not restrain a shiver. "Dumont must have aided him to—"

"Dumont?" Morty scoffed. "Dumont wouldn't have helped him do anything of the sort! Use your head, Billie! Dumont holds most of Kit's vowels. What creditor wishes to see his debtor decamp, especially with the fair chance he might never come back? Oh, don't—don't look like that, Billie! No one of sense will have him anywhere near an actual battle. But Dumont has to be livid. And 'twill bring disgrace on us all. Kit owes thousands! I've just left Esther weeping. She's afraid her father will now refuse the marriage."

"Surely not," Billie ventured. "The debts are Kit's—"

"Devil it! Of course they are! But Father might feel honor-bound to make good. And that means less for the settlements."

"My brother is not a numbskull, Morty," Ephie inserted severely. "He would never be so harebrained as to jeopardize your chance at a match with Miss Urquhart."

"P'rhaps so, Auntie. But *Mother* might prevail upon him to do anything—anything in Kit's interest!" he added bitterly. And wheeling about, he strode, red-faced, from the room. They heard his heavy tread echoing on the hall's marble stairs.

"They are so short of men," Billie said, looking to her aunt. Lord David's comments were fresh in her mind. "Mightn't they simply use Kit wherever they might need him? Even if he is quite unprepared?"

"They are just as likely to punish him, Billie, for failing to obtain proper leave. We must simply wait and see. But do recall that Kit is a good horseman and a fair marksman. Though he is the most ill-disciplined rascal in the world, and clearly lacks necessary sense, he is not so entirely unprepared."

Billie did recall, and tried to set her mind at ease. But the knowledge that two men she held dear were now living at the same threatened Belgian address did not further peaceful slumbers.

The third of June brought a break in the weather and a lawn party at the gorgeous Richmond estate of Lord and Lady Turnbull. Morty, restored to the good graces of his fiancée's family by an assurance that Kit Caswell's debts would in no way affect marriage plans, was once again squiring Esther Urquhart. Morty now seemed oblivious to all but his own contentment. Their father, Sir Moreton, had refused—most surprisingly, in Billie's estimation—to accept that Kit's debts should be met from Morty's intended legacy. Though her father had not gone so far as to deny any obligation on the part of the Caswell family, Sir Moreton had for once—encouragingly and very pointedly—proved deaf to the entreaties of his indulgent lady, who had always chosen to aid the wayward Christopher in everything.

While Morty paraded the Turnbulls' extensive grounds with Esther, Billie and her aunt enjoyed a similar walk with Lord Hayden, who had sought them out upon their arrival. Billie was feeling generous to the greater part of humanity. She had had two days in which to conclude, after frequent readings of his letter, that David intended to renew his suit, and on the basis of the warmest sentiments. Else he would never have written so much so soon after seeing the beauteous Charis. Billie's qualms regarding Kit, Dumont, and Napoléon Bonaparte himself had to be subsidiary.

"You are smiling, Miss Caswell," Hayden remarked. "You find this outing entertaining?"

"I have always preferred to be out-of-doors, my lord. And after such a bout of wet weather, the sun, weak as it is, is particularly welcome."

"It certainly flatters you," he said with a bow to her. "I have never seen you in finer looks."

"I thank you, my lord." She might have suspected Hayden of flummery, but his blue gaze was sincere and guileless. She realized that she rarely looked directly at him, perhaps because those eyes reminded her so disturbingly of his brother.

But he immediately threw her into confusion by asking, "You have heard from David?"

"I have—that is, yes," she managed. "I had a letter from him two days ago."

"He must have been unusually communicative, as I also had word from him two days ago, from Brussels. Perhaps we needn't compare notes." Hayden smiled. "He was certainly well."

"He sounded so."

"And busy about his affairs."

"Yes."

"He had been dining and dancing in the city twice."

"Twice?"

They walked on. The party's lively chatter, now flooding the lawn and drifting out across the river, sounded like the noisy hum of many bees.

"The deprivations and hardship associated with soldiering have never appealed to me," Hayden confessed. "I should be quite out of sorts without lighter detail now and then."

"Certainly," Billie agreed abruptly.

Hayden's eyebrows rose. "You were meant to protest at that, Miss Billie, and assure me that soldiering should suit me admirably."

"Oh, but I meant—my lord, you misunderstood me. Of course I agree that one must understand a soldier's hardships and deprivation."

Again he smiled. "David is a most obliging fellow," he said. "Yes."

"He finds it very difficult to say no."

"Apparently."

Hayden laughed. "You were meant to protest at that as well, Miss Billie. For I assure you that my brother is as stubborn as a man might be. He would not command the hundreds he does if he yielded as easily as that."

Billie glanced away from Hayden's amused gaze and, despite the shade from her bonnet, shielded her eyes as she looked back toward the gaily-decorated party tents, set like a caravan amid an oasis of towering oaks.

"Why do you tease me so, my lord?" she asked.

"Because you mustn't worry," he said simply. "No man ever had a truer heart—should you desire it." Again he bowed to her. And she permitted him to lead her back toward the company. Billie was aware that their amble had been closely observed; Lord Hayden's attentions were always remarked. But it was a large group after all, and Ephie had accompanied them. Billie ignored the speculative glances and proceeded to make her own way across the grass to the site of the archery competition, where she was expected. But May Sanders stopped her.

"Shall one brother do as well as another for you then, Miss Caswell?" she asked pertly. Her tiny hand rested possessively on Lord Grenby's arm. With the comment, Grenby attempted to force an apologetic smile. Again Billie wondered how the gentleman could so promptly transfer his interest from one lady to another, one so entirely different. But that, indeed, was the very essence of May's question.

"My family and that of the Duke of Braughton are Leicestershire neighbors, Miss Sanders," she reminded her.

"Oh, yes, I see!" May said with a laugh, and, pulling upon Grenby's arm, she led him off toward the Turnbulls' famous yew maze.

" 'Tis a most puzzling thing," Ronald Dumont said behind her. "I had credited Grenby with better taste."

Billie wheeled to Dumont. She had scarcely exchanged ten

words with the man, though he had been so frequently in Kit's company this spring. Billie knew him to be a blackguard, a rogue who had so thoroughly entrapped her brother in debt that Billie feared Kit would never be free of him. That in it-self would have made Dumont ugly in her eyes, though in his finery, with his hair carefully coiffed in the Grecian style, he appeared no less a gentleman than anyone else attending the afternoon party. Dumont was easily a decade older than Kit and, in Billie's estimation, should have been honorable enough not to press the younger man's back to the wall.

"Lord Grenby has fine taste," she countered coldly. She thought Dumont's eyes beady. "Miss Sanders is an acknowl-edged Incomparable."

Dumont bowed to her. "But she is not as *incomparable* as his previous interest."

"You presume," she snapped, and turned away from him.

But he stepped closer and blocked her path. "Miss Caswell, your brother has chosen to flee his obligations."

"That is unfortunate, sir, for you. It has nothing whatever to do with me."

"Doesn't it? Should you really like to see Christopher Caswell in filthy Fleet prison?"

"It will not go that far."

"What shall you do to prevent it?"

Billie's hands tightened into fists. For one moment she wished she were again twelve years old and might give the man a hearty shove. She would enjoy ruffling his smooth con-fidence. Instead she fixed him with a glare.

"Do you threaten me?"

"Threaten?" His smile was humorless. "Rather 'offer,' Miss Caswell. Offer you a way to cancel your brother's debts and free the Caswells from disgrace."

"Your 'offer' is the disgrace, Mr. Dumont," she said, under-standing him only too clearly.

Again he smiled. "How delightfully refreshing you are! By

all means, let us be frank, Miss Caswell. I acknowledge my interest in your portion. I also acknowledge that you are beautiful and that I admire your spirit. Should you desire more? Perhaps you would despise me less were I less honest—and pretended to sentiments that you would know to be false."

"I could never despise you less." She watched the blaze of anger settle into his features, but that anger was quickly controlled and masked. "And as for your 'honesty,' you make a mockery of the word, Mr. Dumont. You would describe thieves as 'honest' in their thievery."

As she stepped away from him, he spoke to her back. "Take care you do not trade your brother for your absent major, Miss Caswell."

But Billie refused to turn back. Morty and Esther Urquhart awaited her at the archery pavilion, where several ladies had already fielded their first shots.

"You took your time," Morty muttered. "Here Esther already had to take a turn, and the wind blew her arrow clear away from the target."

Billie forbore to comment, though she'd perceived not the slightest bit of breeze all afternoon. She smiled at Esther, who held the bow as though it might turn viciously upon her.

"Miss Urquhart, do let me see the bow," she offered, taking it from her trembling hands. "There is something wrong here with the tension." Billie made great play of checking it, while Esther sighed in relief and Morty viewed her with a skeptical eye.

"What did Dumont want?" he demanded.

"Nothing," Billie said calmly, glancing at Esther. Sometimes Morty showed no tact. "You must let me try the next shot, Miss Urquhart, as I fear there is a problem with the bow."

Esther gratefully yielded, apparently taking great delight as Billie sent the next arrow flying to the very center of the target, instantly improving the duo's standing.

"Do take the next three as well, Miss Caswell," she urged, "as it's best three of five. And no one said we must split them."

" 'Tis just a game, Miss Urquhart. Everyone who wishes must have a turn."

"Oh, but I should rather win it," Esther conceded. And Billie realized with some surprise that there were possibilities in the demure Miss Urquhart, possibilities of which her staid brother was most probably unaware.

Billie's subsequent two bull's-eyes, though one was rather unsatisfactorily just within bounds, put them in the lead. Perhaps, then, the flush of victory made her bold—or the frustration of knowing that she could not touch the man temporarily robbed her of reason—because Billie pivoted and leveled her remaining arrow at Ronald Dumont, who had been observing the competition from the side of the lawn. She heard Morty's hissed *"Billie!"* and the gasp from those behind her in the crowd. But the satisfaction of holding Dumont captive, even for a moment, was too great to resist.

"I have you in my sights, Mr. Dumont," she challenged.

"I assure you, I am all *aquiver,* Miss Caswell." Despite the pun and his apparent *sangfroid,* Billie thought Dumont's gaze watchful.

She was debating which part of the man might prove more vulnerable—his wizened heart or his evil, calculating head—when a cool hand closed firmly over her tensed fingers, effectively eliminating any risk to either piece of Dumont.

"This is not the way," Hayden said calmly above her head. "Not with one like Dumont."

Across the lawn, Ronald Dumont was laughing, an infuriating sound that made Billie itch to realign her arrow.

"Are you also your brother's keeper, then, Hayden," he called, "that you must be tasked with controlling the ill-tempered cat? I vow you shall find your days numbered."

"Oh, undoubtedly!" Hayden returned easily. "But I must happily bear them, as the lady has graciously consented to become my wife—and my marchioness."

Chapter Ten

Davidsupposed that the evening's duty was better than that of the day before. Rather than standing about a hot roadside in reserve and under fire, they had been tasked with fortifying the defenses of a farmland *château* and its surroundings. The interiors were dry, the men need not anticipate sleeping on the ground, and, given a fortunate dispersion, they would have a roof over their heads for the night. As the rain had fallen unrelentingly since the afternoon's thunderstorm, the roof would be a luxury.

David had seen the place several times during the past three months while traveling outside his billet in Enghien. The *château* Hougoumont—"Gum Hill"—was very near two major roads south from Brussels, en route to the towns of Nivelles and Charleroi on the French border. As the countryside had been on alert for weeks for signs of incursions by Bonaparte and his troops, the area was much reviewed. He, in fact, had been one of many to review it.

Yet Bonaparte's initial thrust had still surprised them. Wellington had even been heard to claim that the French emperor had "humbugged" him. Wellington and his staff had been caught off guard; indeed, word was that many had been pulled abruptly, at an early hour of the morning, from the Duchess of Richmond's ball in Brussels. David, thankfully, had not attended the ball—he'd had no interest in attending, despite a plea from Miss Athington.

The allied forces had been set into motion by moonlight—to gather south of Brussels near the crossroads at Quatre Bras, in an effort to counter the French. David and the Household Guards, including some of his own regiment of infantry, the Coldstream, had marched nearly twenty-five miles—to stand there in the hot sun amid tall fields of rye and corn—and coolly hope that artillery fire overshooting the battle south of them did not strike their ranks. Even when the order had come that the men might lie down, and David had dismounted, there had still been casualties, though there had been no enemy at which to fire. The troops he had accompanied had not been called to the front line, though Captain Bowles' company had. They had *heard* much from the clash ahead of them, but the thriving grain had obscured almost all. The only evidence of battle had been the noise and the casualties passing to the rear along the road. That had been enough to make the newer recruits pale.

David himself did not fear the fighting; he simply wished it over. Yet it was not to be over soon.

Though Wellington had not "lost" at Quatre Bras, the result of the previous day's engagement had to be considered inconclusive. The allies had been victorious along the roadway; by late afternoon Bowles' Coldstream unit had even moved in front of the contested farmhouse south of the crossroads. But their allies, the Prussians under Field Marshal von Blücher, had been defeated farther east, at Ligny. The Prussians had lost at least 14,000 infantry and cavalry. Panicked survivors—or perhaps they were deserters—had raced back to Brussels with the news that Bonaparte had "won"—that the allies were doomed. Seasoned veteran of the Peninsular war that he was, David knew that more was to come.

Wellington's forces had pulled back another eight miles toward Brussels and the north, attempting to present a seamless, united front with the damaged Prussians, who had retreated to the east—to the town of Wavre. Along a ridge of land stretching east and west of the village of Mont St. Jean, Wellington dispersed the allied army to shield Brussels: British regiments mostly to the west, guarding supply lines toward the Channel; and Belgians, Dutch, and Germans to the east, in hopes that they would eventually be supplemented by Blücher's returning army.

The Hougoumont farm, forward and to the west of Wellington's center, could not be let to fall to the French, or Bonaparte would flank the allied army and cut off its supplies. So the allies had laid claim first, and they intended to hold.

David found the place eminently defensible. The residence and a small private chapel stood at the heart of a pair of inner courtyards, protected on the west by stables and a huge barn, on the south by offices and garden buildings, and on the north by several cowsheds. Most of the buildings were of weathered gray stone. To the east lay an elaborate formal garden, bounded by sturdy brick walls, and beyond that an extensive orchard, surrounded on all sides by a thick, high hedge. A sunken farm lane bounded the north side of the farm.

David thought his cousin Chas, who designed landscapes, would certainly have recognized the terrain as a strong point. And Chas would have found much charming in the site, though the buildings, serving the practical interests of the farm, were too closely positioned to allow for grand vistas. Chas might also have found the formal garden too strictly confined—David could well imagine him speaking of "opening it up."

Indeed, the garden was likely to be opened up, but not in a good way.

David suspected that it was indirectly due to Chas' influence that he was here at all. The few phrases of German his cousin had managed to teach him years ago gave him more of the language than most—enough to give some direction and nod an occasional approving *"ausgezeichnet"*—"excellent!"— to the German troops, who were from Nassau and Hanover.

Should any of them decide to cut and run, David hoped the desertion would not be at his instigation, from some misunderstanding.

He rather grimly set about helping to direct the light company and a battalion of Nassauers in making improvements to the farm's defenses—for one, making loopholes in the gray stone walls of the buildings, a tedious task for men with little more than a few pickaxes and spare farm implements. Outside, where the south-side garden brick wall topped David's better than six-foot height, a firing platform had to be constructed so that men might aim muskets over the wall as well as through loopholes carved out with bayonets. Luckily, a mature wood south of the farm screened Hougoumont from artillery fire on that side. But lacking much in the way of undergrowth, the wood offered little protection for the men who would initially be assigned to defend it. Still, they must start with positions in the wood and outside the farm, only falling back upon their defenses if necessary. There was no point in surrendering ground before it might be wrenched away.

All of these tasks would have been much easier without the unremitting downpour. But recalling that rain had preceded almost all Wellington's victories on the Peninsula, David indulged in some reassuring superstition. From inside the building, the sound of rain upon the tiled roof was even pleasant.

As he circulated, he heard the men speaking of matters of little import: a renowned boxing mill at home, a well-trained dog, beloved qualities of the best ales. He knew they kept a lid upon their feelings and directed their thoughts from the upcoming struggle.

"What is this place, Major?" one of them asked as they worked. "Who lives here?"

"I cannot say. I've spotted smoke from the chimneys whenever I've passed, but I've only ever seen farmworkers about. 'Tis a nice place for the area, though somewhat less than a castle. As the owners appear to have departed, leaving the house without a stick of furniture, we will consider it ours—and hold it as such."

That brought smiles to their faces. Possession was more than half the battle. And they were likely to be seriously outnumbered. But there were British cannons on the ridge behind them, where the allied forces held their main position. The guns would help protect their flanks.

Since Bonaparte had not, unexpectedly, pursued them that day, Wellington had had time to settle his army along the ridge, masking men and artillery on the reverse slope—a tactic that had served him well in the Peninsula. And the element of surprise, having been exercised the day before by the French, was no longer with their adversary.

Despite the rain, despite the fact that it was almost midsummer, David found himself thinking of the New Year at Braughton, of the ball and of Billie Caswell. He suspected that his letter to her must have read as incoherent. He certainly felt incoherent; in fact, he feared the girl made him silly. At the moment he could ill afford to feel silly, but he recalled the New Year nonetheless. And he wondered, for the hundredth time, why he had not heard from her. He had not believed her so particular in her manners. At that ball, he had declared himself. He sensed he did not misread *her*. But perhaps concerns for her family had intruded once more. . . .

"What is that you hum, Major?" Corporal Crosby, who had known him for years in Spain and Portugal, looked amused.

"Was I humming, Corporal?"

"You were, sir. A carol. A Christmas carol."

"I've a notion, Crosby, that we shall soon be eager enough to recall winter—when events here are engaging us warmly." And, pleased with the eased expressions of the men and with his impromptu excuse, David fled the crew at the south gate, to go inspect the garden wall.

His cap and greatcoat kept him reasonably dry. Occasionally he passed under the shelter of a tree. From the top of the firing platforms one could see just over the wall, across an open grassy stretch about eighty feet wide, to the woods. Those firing from the platforms would have to keep their heads down whenever possible. But anyone attacking against the wall would be at a distinct disadvantage.

David did not know if he was to stay here with Hougoumont's defenders. He had, he considered now, rather mindlessly passed on promotion in order to stay with his regiment of foot. Yet here he was employed just as though promoted, floating—as coordinator, translator—instead of aide-de-camp, his previous role. Wellington did not stand on ceremony. If it served him, he might treat a captain like a general; he had no second in command. David would wait to see what was required of him in the morning.

British artillery on the ridge behind the farm sent word that two French corps had drawn up south of the wood, indicating that the French had perceived the importance of the *château* to their opponents' defenses. In response, the Nassauers were sent into that wood, to meet the earliest onslaughts of French infantry, anticipated with daylight. Additional skirmishers, consisting of a light company of Coldstreamers, Third Foot Guardsmen, and more Nassauers, were tasked with defending a small, hedged kitchen garden outside the western perimeter of the barn. As the night advanced, David spent much of it walking along the lane dividing the barn from that garden and the fields and occasionally passing into the courtyards where other Nassauers were dispersed. By standing sentry, he decided he was minimally more comfortable than the Coldstream skirmishers, most of whom had bivouacked, grumbling, in the mud.

By the northwest gate, where a small pond lay in the shade of elm trees, the night's flood of rain gradually created a marsh.

At some early hour of the morning, perhaps two or three, David woke from an hour of sleep upon a loft's bed of straw.

The French had moved into the wood, encountering a patrol of the Germans, who quickly routed them. But the success was too early and too small to quell anticipation of a massive engagement later in the morning. Out again in the kitchen garden before dawn, David missed Wellington's brief visit to Hougoumont, a visit that indicated the importance in which the allied commander held the farm. David managed to swallow some tea and a proffered bowl of "stirrabout," the mens' simple oatmeal porridge. Despite the mists and continuing clouds, the morning was drier; he might otherwise have considered it promising, but it could hardly seem so under the circumstances. Half a mile in the distance, visible from the upper floors in the *château,* French banners and massed men and horses covered the rise of ground beyond the grain fields to the southeast. By contrast, the allied army, upon the ridge behind them, was hardly visible. Oddly, their immediate enemy—the French troops beyond the wood immediately to Hougoumont's south—could not be seen at all. But everyone knew they were there; they had heard the Nassauers' encounter and musket fire in the wee hours.

As that Sunday morning progressed, the anomaly was that nothing further occurred. David had expected Bonaparte, in the emperor's usual bold manner, to attack with daylight, yet the stillness continued.

The *château* was prepared; there was little else they could do to buttress their small garrison, except to maintain their confidence. David knew the farm held some of the army's best troops, at least the most experienced. He himself was so experienced that he was rather curiously optimistic. Before a battle he was never certain whether to ascribe his calm to having been tested or to hard-earned fatalism.

Before noon Wellington again visited Hougoumont, with the liaison for the Prussian army, General Muffling. David thought he overheard Muffling telling the duke that the place, forward of its own army's lines, could not be held.

When the duke then looked directly at David, he promptly responded, unaware that he spoke in French, "It can be held, Your Grace."

"We are no longer in Paris, Trent," Wellington noted in some amusement. "You might speak English—if you wish to preserve a whole skin today."

David could laugh along with the other officers. Wellington had always preferred relaxed high spirits about him. And his French was excellent; he and David had habitually conversed in the language during the fall and winter in Paris.

One of the other officers asked why Bonaparte had not yet attacked.

"I shouldn't question it, Colonel," Wellington responded. "He might take as long as he wishes this morning. All the better for us." And every man there knew their commander referred to the need to have Blücher's Prussian army, still away to the east, join them.

"Trent," Wellington said as he left, "take yourself up to the brigade on the ridge. I'm asking Saltoun and his First Foot to do the same. You shall know soon enough if we must reinforce this place."

Even as David promptly set off to pull Incendio from the stable in the south offices, he fought his frustration. To spend all night helping to fortify the farm—only to hand it over to the Nassauers! But he knew he might as easily have been directed to the other end of the allied line. As he followed shortly after the duke's own departure through the north gate, he advised two privates attending it to shut it behind him.

"But, sir, we was told to keep it open for supplies and such," one of them responded.

"Surely you can tell the difference, man? Open it as needed. There's little call to give the French a hearty welcome."

"Aye, Major."

David galloped out under the elms and up the rain-soaked slope to the other Coldstream companies. Less than half an hour after he'd transferred to the main position, French guns opened engagement, booming across the valley with a terrific roar. The allied artillery answered in turn. At least five batteries of French guns could be seen to the south of Hougoumont, yet they were set to firing upon the allied line instead of the farm. The woods just beyond the farm were alive with the blasts of musketry, where the Nassauers would be fighting to retain their forward position against astonishing numbers of French infantry. With his telescope David could see, even amid all the gunpowder smoke, the German troops break the cover of the woods and flee to the orchard and farmyards. But as soon as the French attempted to follow suit and break the cover of the trees, they became targets along the south side grassy lane, taking devastating fire from the south gate and muskets positioned along the garden wall. Though some French managed to reach the large orchard on the east, they were soon driven back. Thus David watched an initial assault upon Hougoumont end, with its defenses of the previous night having held. Wellington need not risk drawing backup forces from the center of the allied line—yet.

The noise from the guns and the responding fire was deafening. Positioned as they were in reserve behind Hougoumont, David and the First and Coldstream regiments were somewhat protected by the farm and trees. But men fell from artillery strikes nonetheless, as they were standing on the forward slope of the ridge and could not break rank.

David was next aware of a clash to the west of the farm, where the French must have made a move to outflank it. The light company of Coldstream infantry, who had retained the kitchen garden to the west of the barn since the previous night, were now being pushed back to the north gate. Overwhelmed by their attackers, the British troops fled inside to the courtyard, only to be closely followed by the French.

"Blast!" David fumed aloud. "Close that bloody gate!" About thirty French troops had spilled into the courtyard.

More French were massed on the west side of the farm, attempting to outflank the allied position. The British guns behind them were trained to the west but could do nothing about the gate itself without risking hitting the defenders. The gates began to close, even as David and the colonel of his regiment, Colonel Woodford, raced down with their companies to clear the French threatening the north side of the farm. With a furious will and effort to repulse them, they drove the French away from the gate area, completely around the west side of the barn, and back into the woods.

David reentered the farm with the reinforcing companies of British infantry and helped disperse them throughout the buildings and garden. Already there were wounded men inside the stables and barn, but they could not be removed while further assaults were expected. The day was growing hot. David made certain the wounded were receiving water and downed a cup himself. He learned that Colonel McDonnell, whom Wellington had placed in command at Hougoumont, had personally helped close the north gate amid that last intrusion.

Behind the gate and cowsheds the inner courtyard was now covered in the bodies of the blue-coated Frenchmen who had dared to enter the farm. Only one French uniform remained upright, that of a young drummer boy, the only one spared. He looked shocked.

"Would you speak with him, Major?" a beefy sergeant asked. "He doesn't speak English."

David nodded and introduced himself to the lad, who could hardly be treated as a prisoner. Nor could he be considered a combatant, for he had lost even his drum. He said his name was Guillaume.

"Ah, another 'Billie,'" David muttered aloud. "And more trouble." He had to fight a sudden flood of memory.

He handed the boy the carefully preserved lumps of sugar that were Incendio's treat after every battle. At first the boy eyed the sweet suspiciously. He tentatively licked one lump.

But he was soon relishing it. As David led him to the south courtyard, thinking to lodge him with the gardener, who had, inconceivably, wished to stay with his young daughter at the farm, David asked distractedly about the boy's home in France. But his mind was on the battle still raging about them; he knew there was worse to come.

"I shall come back for you," he told the boy, who, despite stroking Incendio's black muzzle with care and apparent calm, looked permanently wide-eyed. The youth had already seen more of war that morning than most men saw in a lifetime.

David reentered the formal garden. As he approached the eastern wall, fronting the orchard, the guards defending it started firing. The French, having hacked through part of the hedge, were attempting to invade the orchard.

Seeing that the French aimed to bypass the farm through the orchard, David sent men to reinforce the wall at the southeast corner, where the brick wall met the hedge. From behind Hougoumont, Lord Saltoun's First Foot guardsmen swept in to confront the French in the orchard, the Guards fighting their way forward beneath the apple trees, compelling the French to return to the woods, to which they now laid claim.

As he turned back to the *château* buildings, David stepped upon one flimsy firing platform and quickly popped up to look over at the grassy strip beyond the wall. The lane was strewn with the dead, even as close as the wall itself, where some, attempting to scale the brick, had been bayoneted.

Three assaults, David thought, moving briskly back to the south gate, *and still we hold.*

Behind him, at the center of the allied line, the noise from artillery, firing guns, and the screams and yells of men amounted to a roar. Little more than a thousand yards separated Hougoumont from the next farm, La Haye Sainte. That farm was just forward of the allied center, where Wellington kept watch with his staff. David knew that if the thousand yards of fields between them looked anything like the greenway south of Hougoumont, this gentle valley would soon be covered in corpses rather than crops.

From the south-facing offices, a cry went up that the French had brought forward a heavy gun, a howitzer, right to the edge of the wood. It was remarkable that the French had not attempted to bring up such a gun before now; a howitzer's high trajectory might reach them, where cannon fire could not. A company of Guards rushed at the threat, but they were forced back into the orchard. Emboldened, the French renewed their attacks upon the garden, where the Nassauers and British infantry were compelled to fight like skirmishers in close combat over the wall. But steady musket fire kept the French howitzer from being manned.

There was little need for orders under the circumstances. Though there was much confusion, all the men had something tangible to defend, at all costs and at any point. They were not to fall back. When, in the offices above the south gate, a guardsman slumped to the floor beside him, wounded by a ball shot through a window, David grabbed the man's gun and headed out again to the garden wall. At an open loophole he fired at movement in the woods across the lane. The musket volley along the wall was so unrelentingly intense that the French howitzer had to be pulled back.

David passed the musket on to a young soldier whose own weapon had jammed. Word passed along the length of the wall that Lord Saltoun's Guards had again moved to clear the orchard. In the smoke and press of men, one could see little beyond forty or fifty feet, so David had to believe, or hope, that the relayed message was accurate. In the next lull, at midafternoon—with the orchard again reclaimed, Saltoun's forces drawn back to the allied line, and not an inch of the garden or courtyards lost—David set men to work removing the wounded to the interiors of the buildings.

He thought the French, even to pause so long, must have

thought they'd successfully killed every one of them. But the interlude was not to last. One of the men David had sent to the end of the garden, to report on the state of the orchard, returned to say that it was still theirs, but that new columns of French infantry had been sighted marching across the field of battle, from the French center, heading for Hougoumont. Fortunately, the British guns on the ridge behind them easily fired on this new threat as it dared to cross so boldly in the open, in front of the allied position, and no French infantry reached the orchard to eject the newly resident Third regiment of foot.

Even as David heard this heartening report, a shell or some flaming debris landed atop the roof of the thatched barn, serving then like a match to ignite the surrounding buildings, which erupted into a blaze. The west stable, the small chapel, and even the tile-roofed *château* itself were soon engulfed. David anticipated more such missiles. Though none followed, the effect of the one was pervasive and deadly.

Confronting the triple tasks of avoiding further risks from the fires, maintaining the farm's defenses, and removing the wounded men he had earlier placed inside the now-crumbling buildings, David worked quickly and desperately to save as many as he could. What was supposed to have been best shielded and safest had become a death trap. He and a team of others pulled several wounded from the large cart house just before the roof fell in, entombing those remaining. With faces blackened by soot and gunpowder and streaked with sweat, every man in the place still defended the torched ruins. Despite the consuming flames and ovenlike heat of the afternoon, despite the suffocating smoke, not a man left his post at the outer walls or inside the tottering buildings. The French might have destroyed the place, David thought grimly, but they would not possess the charred remains.

Even as Hougoumont burned, at midafternoon a brave Royal wagon train driver raced down to the north gate, bringing them more ammunition from up at the line. Though the driver lost his horses to furious French fire, he supplied the soldiers with the musket balls that had flown so unremittingly. They were, David thought, the only currency between Hougoumont's contenders.

The stifling afternoon wore on. French attention appeared to be drawn to the center of the battlefield, giving David and the others an opportunity to reconnoiter. The wounded were removed to the south-side buildings that remained intact, and, in an effort to plug gaps, muskets and ammunition were redistributed from slain guardsmen along the garden walls. The deafening artillery from the fight to their east was such a constant accompaniment that it resolved itself into a hum. One could not shut out the groans of those injured and dying. Though David knew there should be at least two surgeons with his own regiment, he did not know where they were to be found. And at any moment the French might be relied upon to renew their assault.

The men were cleaning their muskets. David pulled more wounded men from the garden, placing some in the small stable where Incendio and the few remaining horses were saddled and ready. Across from that stable, the once elegant *château* stood, only a shell in flames.

"Steady, fellow," David muttered, rubbing his black charger's muzzle just as the French drummer boy had done earlier. Little Guillaume, hovering near, appeared to have more color in his cheeks. He asked David how much longer he must stay.

"A few more hours, *mon ami*," David said, and he repeated the words more softly to Incendio. Through the open stable door he could see that the base of the chapel was now blazing. Across the garden, upon the slope to the ridge, the 52nd regiment had formed two squares just off the northeast corner of Hougoumont. French cavalry had begun charging those squares and others, unseen upon the ridge, probably in the mistaken notion that Wellington had pulled his army back. Instead, David knew his commander was likely to be preserving his forces from French artillery by moving them behind the rise.

Even as he questioned the fate of Alan Athington and others he knew in the 52nd, even as he watched the French cavalry charge repeatedly, David turned his weary attention to the tasks at hand. Again he entered the garden.

"Bitte—" a young Nassauer choked, as he lay upon crushed herbs and vegetables in the once neatly plotted beds. David offered the German his own canteen, holding the injured man's head up as he scarcely managed a sip before expiring. There were too many like him; the fighting had been fierce and prolonged. Many had struggled for hours with wounds from the first attacks, only to succumb now in the relative calm.

David ran the length of the garden wall along the south and east of the garden. When he met his colonel, Woodford, and McDonnell, he heard that Wellington had noticed the fires at Hougoumont and had sent a note desiring that men be spared from the flames, but stressing that the farm must remain theirs. The duke had been answered with an assurance. And the chapel still stood, though the blaze had risen as high as the feet of a wooden figure of Jesus inside the door.

David thought it a curiosity that after despairing of so much rain the night before, and though the mists and damp had persisted, he should now feel so thirsty. Given the carnage and devastation about him, it was strange to feel anything other than numbed. But he did crave water. He set a subaltern to collecting canteens from the dead and portioning the water to the men at the wall. There was a well in the north farmyard, but even that seemed too far away.

Again they waited. David could no longer distinguish how many attacks had been rebuffed. He recognized only that this had been a ferocious bit of fighting.

Early in the evening, the French infantry took advantage of its own cavalry movements, not to support that cavalry but to

make yet another dedicated invasion of Hougoumont's orchard. As the French swarmed onto the ground, David stayed
at the east garden wall and watched Hepburn's Third Foot
Guards fight valiantly before being forced to give way.

"There is more French, sir," one frustrated Nassauer remarked in broken English, furiously reloading his musket, "than
we are."

"Yes," David agreed. "But we have walls."

They gave the French no chance to press an advantage. The
German troops and Coldstreamers along the east wall kept up
such a thick and fierce barrage of musketry fire that the apple
trees themselves started to waver, their branches hanging
limply. The Third's soldiers were able to recover and evict the
invaders. But there was no time for celebration. The exercise
was repeated: the French again moved in from the east side of
the orchard, the British infantry were pushed back to the
sunken road, and then the defenders at the garden wall, muskets blazing, pummeled the persistent French. On both sides
the troops were nearing a state of exhaustion. This time, when
the British Guards counterattacked through the trees, the
French appeared set to vacate the orchard for good. The soggy
ground under the orchard's rows was covered in red, blue, and
green uniforms. But now, pressing forward to the far hedge at
the east side of the orchard, Hougoumont's champions could
fire into the French cavalry's flanks.

It was early evening. The light was beginning to fade.
David did not anticipate another attack. After such continu-
ous, defiant effort, not one part of Hougoumont, even the
much-disputed orchard, had been lost to Bonaparte's forces,
though the remaining buildings and scorched surroundings
were now scarcely recognizable. Not an inch had been lost,
but it seemed to David that almost every inch was covered in
some form of devastation. On his return to the south yard, he
had to make his way past men dead and dying, German and

British. He might have spent hours simply tending to the wounded.

He learned that the other farm, La Haye Sainte, having failed to receive a resupply of ammunition, had fallen to the French, inspiring the attackers to new efforts. But the allied center upon the ridge held firm. Bonaparte would be compelled to desperate measures if he were to carry the day. Yet the French emperor still had a chance at victory, because the much-looked-for Prussian army had still not arrived to strengthen the allies.

The French cavalry's fierce charges appeared to have ended. Since the other British Guards regiments had been pulled back to support the line up upon the ridge, the slope behind Hougoumont now hosted replacement companies of Hanoverians and the King's German Legion. After consulting with the other officers, David was tasked with informing their new German reinforcements of the state of the farm. So he retrieved Incendio, in the process cautioning little Guillaume to wait for his return. Passing through the farm's north gate with a number of walking wounded, David made his way to the east, along the sunken way, then turning to move gradually upslope. There, more wounded British Guards, resting from the battles in the orchard, sat about looking physically spent. The fighting had been at close quarters, often with bayonet. In the absence of aid, the wounded were attempting to look after one another.

David could at last see more of the valley, at least that part on the allied right side. In the press of battle, with the limited views, he had not comprehended just how many men had confronted one another today within a small, suffocating space. The reality was appalling. The armies were so dense, they looked not like men but waves, moving in currents across the rain-soaked, undulating ground—a great, grinding swell of sweating, bloodied, muddy humanity. The morning's shoulder-high crops had been so trampled and crushed that they now resembled reed mats, a peculiar terrestrial flotsam cushioning the casualties.

He had never seen such a slaughter. He hoped never to see it again. What had seemed like the world to him for so many intense hours at Hougoumont had been only part of this blasted whole.

He spoke briefly with a captain of Du Plat's King's German Legion, which regiment thankfully gave its orders in English, and then with a lieutenant of Colonel Halkett's Hanoverians, relaying to both the state of Hougoumont and hearing in turn their news of Wellington and the line. Prepared to go back, David turned about. As he neared a short hedge and low bank just forward of one of the 52nd infantry's vacated squares, he heard a sharp groan. Peering under the thick holly and beech hedge, he spotted several figures lying still, and their uniforms were red.

"Trent!" one of them croaked, before lapsing into ragged coughs.

David dismounted instantly. Drawing Incendio behind him, he moved closer to the hedge and knelt to look into a muddy face framed by a blanket.

"Athington!"

Chapter Eleven

"Athington! What do you do here?"

Again Alan Athington groaned. "Put here—ahead of square. No time—take us—rear—"

"Your wounds are bad?"

Athington nodded. "Others . . ."

David checked the two other men. Neither breathed.

"They are gone, Athington. You cannot stay here. I must take you up to the line. You see I have my horse."

"No . . . time," he said. "Do you not . . . hear it?"

The guns were still firing. Seemingly the day's cannonading had left David deaf. But in the distance he could just hear the faintest drumbeat. *Ta-rum-dum, ta-rum-dum, ta-rum-a-dum, rum-a-dum, dum, dum.* The beat repeated across the bloody, darkening valley. It was the French *pas de charge.* In the last hour before the sun set, Bonaparte was sending his tried and trusted personal guard, the Imperial Guard, against the allied line.

"Look out . . . for Caswell," Athington muttered. "He stopped . . . in our square."

"Caswell!" David was hauling the boy out from under the hedge. "You mean the captain? Jack Caswell?"

Athington's dark gaze was unfocused. "Kit. Junior ADC. General Smallwood. Think . . . friend of . . . family. Kit . . . shammed it." Again he struggled through a cough. "Jumped . . . inside our square . . . just before hit."

David was attempting, gently, to right him. Athington was heavier than he looked. But he could not be left there. The drumbeats sounded louder.

"I shall keep an eye out. But, Athington, where are you wounded?"

"Right arm—right leg. You must . . . cosh me, on the head. Less . . . painful."

The lad had bottom. David raised him and steadied him against Incendio's side, then strained to shove him up across the saddle. He had to move, and quickly.

As he urged Incendio up the slope, he thought Athington might have swooned. But then he was talking again, and garrulously.

"Guess he's still . . . in-law. But not . . . the same—what?" He started to laugh but halted, hacking.

"I don't understand you, man," David said tightly. To hear wild chatter now distracted him. He probably should have ridden on—officers were reprimanded for stopping—but he had never quite been able to do it. . . .

"Hayden . . . marryin' Miss Caswell. In the *Times* . . . last week."

"That's nonsense, Athington," he bit out. "Miss Caswell is to marry me."

"Not . . . no longer. Sanders girl—wrote Charis. M'sister's . . . never wrong." He drew a ragged breath. "Shouldn't mind . . . you as . . . brother, Trent. . . ."

Handsome of you, David thought. But he said aloud, and curtly, "You're off your head, Athington. Don't talk anymore. Here." He wedged one of the lieutenant's boots into a stirrup, then rearranged the muddy blanket. Given his gentler breathing, Athington must have passed out.

David looked behind them. He could now see the Imperial Guard, Bonaparte's Middle Guard, marching toward them in the dusk. Amid the drumbeats he heard the cries of *"Vive l'Empereur! Vive l'Empereur!"* The column was impressive—uniformly tall, matchlessly disciplined, dedicated, and intimidating. They looked a race of giants.

He hurried Incendio on, as well as they could in such a carpet of dead and dying, and crested the first bank bordering the ridge's sunken road. They crossed the road and mounted the farther bank, to find a quietly prone army of guardsmen lying in wait on the reverse side of the bank. Farther behind them was a confusion of wagons and horses and reserves, civilians, even women and children, searching for injured soldiers, calling in efforts to locate regiments—or taking the opportunity to steal the effects of the wounded and dead. The volume of activity behind the lines was amazing. Yet somehow David's batman, Barton, found him in that melee.

"I saw you—makin' your way up the slope, m'lord—Major," he gasped. He'd been running. "I feared you'd be caught in the firing."

David shook his head. "I'll ask you, Barton, to take Lieutenant Athington to shelter." He was, as carefully as possible, sliding Athington from Incendio's back. "Find him a doctor." David slid a hand inside his tunic to remove his watch. "Take this, should you need to pay for help or a bed. And keep Athington's things as well. I'm back to the farm. You might find me there tonight." He could tell that Barton had no fondness for the task. His duty, as he had always seen it, was to look after the major, not to tend the major's friends.

David smiled at him. " 'Twill all come right, Barton." And he watched his faithful servant gulp hard before hoisting Athington upon his broad and capable shoulders.

David remounted Incendio and rode westward along the bank. He was not meant to be up here; he prepared to move back down the slope to Hougoumont. But as he again crossed the road and essayed to climb over the forward-facing bank, his gaze caught a flailing red-sleeved arm thirty paces downslope, amid the disheartening debris and growing dimness. A dozen French cavalry incursions had clearly taken a severe toll upon the line, though no squares had been broken. The British continued to fire artillery at the approaching French guard, but David knew that the firing would have to cease as the French came closer. Remembering Athington, convinced that the waving arm was in some way a signal, a supplication, he spurred Incendio down the slope.

He was made to act; he had always acted. Invariably, when he had failed to do so, he had found himself regretting.

British shells and grape struck just beyond him. As he slid from the saddle, he found Kit Caswell, apparently intact but wedged between a dead horse and an equally dead French cavalry *cuirassier* in all his heavy armor. Kit's eyes were closed. His flailing arm must have moved merely in spasm, because the boy now looked still. He certainly felt cold enough. But that face! David could not have left that familiar face out there. And for a wounded man to be left amid this multitude was akin to a sentence of death.

With a disheartened sense that Kit Caswell was doomed if not yet dead, David summoned a strength he had not believed he retained, rolling the French *cuirassier* off Kit's side and pulling him from beneath the horse. The *rum-a-dum* of the French drums burned his ears. But he blessed the fading light and the confused detritus of battle about him, which hid his actions. The French columns were not yet close enough to fire—and, at that, they were unlikely to waste their shot upon just one horse and rider. Nothing else was visible to them. The cries of *"Vive l'Empereur!"* echoed loudly.

Kit was lighter than Athington. Incendio stood still as David tossed the boy upon the horse and hauled him toward the ridge, the mud sucking greedily at his boots. At the first bank, in the growing dusk, he pulled Incendio farther along the rise before dropping behind it, lest he reveal the fortified dip to the French guards in the lead.

Swiftly David tore off his coat and forced Kit's arms into it, leaving it loose and unbuttoned about him. The boy was so cold he had to be in shock, but he had a pulse. The coat might help—Kit's own was in tatters—and David knew that high officers received closer attention than the rank and file. He ripped a blanket from a fallen pack and wrapped that around Kit as well, then propped him upright in the saddle. Hastily he tied Kit's boots to the stirrups with his own belt, and, flattening Kit against Incendio's mane, loosely tethered his hands about the horse's neck.

"Well, you won't fall off," David said grimly. Kit mumbled indistinctly. David had seen no blood on the boy, but he had to have broken bones or internal damage of an extensive nature to be so limp and cold.

Behind them and to the left, David saw the French formation march right up to the crest of the ridge, right to a wall of corpses. At some word down the line—some order that David could not hear—the Guards hiding there behind the far bank leapt to their feet and unleashed a barrage of fire into the column of French. David saw the French surprise and dismay, not in their faces but in their actions. Some still attempted to move forward, some halted to return fire, and some were so startled and staggered they were attempting to turn, even in the close formation.

"La Garde recule!" David yelled, thinking to add to their confusion. *"La Garde recule!"* The Guard retreats! As the cry was picked up and repeated in panic, David slapped Incendio's flank hard, sending the horse and Kit galloping toward the rear of the line. *I hope, Kit Caswell,* he thought, *you might make her some amends.*

As well as he could then, David ran, down into the road and across it. Sir John Colborne's 52nd regiment stood there in column, firing upon the French. As David moved behind them, he saw Wellington approach on horseback along the ridge, once again foolishly—but magnificently, *inspiringly*—exposing himself to enemy fire.

"Go on!" Wellington urged Colborne. "Go on! They won't

stand!" And the 52nd advanced downhill, astonishingly swinging into a parade-ground-perfect line formation, to close like a
hinge upon the French west flank. David had never seen a maneuver of its like. Though devastating to the inflexibly tight
French column, the movement also exposed the 52nd in an un-
common way. They would take high casualties. In the muck
and growing darkness, David hurried to alert the German
companies behind Hougoumont not to fire mistakenly into the
backs of the 52nd.

His legs felt heavy; they did not wish to advance him. He
was exhausted, wearied to numbness. Without Incendio, it
was difficult to get about. And in outfitting Kit Caswell, he
had abandoned his sword. He had not used it all day—he suspected he would scarcely have had strength to raise it—but it
might have served as support in the mud. Now, reduced to his
shirtsleeves, he was chilled, though the battleground had earlier felt like an oven. He found a sodden blanket, more mud
than wool, and slung it about his shoulders. When he reached
an officer of Halkett's Hanoverian brigade, the man looked
upon him in astonishment but recognized his face. By a com-
bination of hand gestures and the simplest of vocabulary,
David tried to convey that a line of British infantry now stood
between their brigade and the French guard. The lieutenant
seemed to understand, and indicated that in any advance his
forces would be moving south to retake the woods beyond
Hougoumont.

David strode on, down to the KGL brigade, to quickly
communicate the same. But as he left them, heading for the
sunken lane behind Hougoumont, something exploded, seemingly straight up from the ground. David felt a glance, as
though of an impact, yet his arms and legs were still intact. As
he looked down he could see them, and his mud-spattered
shirt, still white in the dusk. A Hanoverian trooper had trailed
him for some reason and now came to his side, grasping his arm
and gesticulating earnestly. The man was saying something to

him, something in incomprehensibly mangled German and English. David thought bemusedly that theirs was certainly a mad and motley army—expected to move in concert, when they could not even understand one another! His mind seemed unusually slow. He recognized the word *granate,* repeated several times. But no one used grenades anymore. A shell, perhaps. Or did the fool mistake him for a French Grenadier? Then, *schlecht.* Bad. Yes, this was all very bad. But why the devil had he been stopped?

Impatiently he shook off the German's hand and started to walk. There was something dreamlike about the smoldering ruins of Hougoumont before him, the thick dark smoke, the looming hedge, the last few rays of light from the fading sun reflecting eerily in the broken clouds. When he reached the sunken road, he abruptly, unexpectedly, fell to his knees, and looked down at the soft mud with an astonished laugh. What a fine commander he was—to be incapable of standing upright at the end of the day!

The French boy, "Billie," his little blue coat still too clearly distinguishable in the dusk, was creeping toward him along the sunken path.

"You were to wait for me!" David shouted in French. His voice cracked, from hours of yelling, and despite his alarm the thought struck him as hilarious. For some inexplicable reason he was laughing. "This way is dangerous! Go back!" The boy came on, though David was certain he had shouted. He believed he had heard himself shout. But something—a musket ball—struck his left shoulder. The wrong direction . . . from the King's own German legion, begad! *These many nervous recruits* . . . But with the sharp sting, all else blanked.

Number 16, St. James's Square, the elegant residence of Mr. and Mrs. Boehm, was brightly lit and beautifully decorated for the night's assembly. The evening had been anticipated as the most brilliant of the waning season. Yet the glittering company outshone the surroundings. Many distinguished personages, including the Prince Regent and his brother, the Duke of York, were to attend.

Since the Richmond picnic, Billie and Hayden had ventured out together only infrequently—to a few dinner parties, two dances, another musicale—but gossip had been rife nonetheless. Hayden was always a much sought after, most elusive guest. That he should now trouble to attend events, and with a fiancée, was something to be noted with excitement.

Billie entered the Boehms' on Hayden's arm. This dance was by far the largest event they had attended together. She felt the weight of attention, the many gazes curious and assessing. She knew that Hayden was much studied and emulated and that he was invariably discussed, whereas she had no wish to be the same.

"You tire of this, my dear," he observed softly. He was looking to the crowd as he spoke.

"'Tis all most . . . invigorating, I know, my lord. And I am truly grateful. . . ." As his steady gaze turned to hers, she stopped and said frankly, "I find this trickery wearing. The deception."

"Yes," he sighed. "You would."

She thought she heard the slightest emphasis on the *you.* Billie looked at him sharply. "It does not trouble *you?*"

"Not unduly, Miss Caswell. Deception is the oil of society, after all. Without it, we should all sink." And as though to illustrate the truth of the remark, he turned to compliment a lady who had approached him, a lady who seemed overly willing to believe Hayden's flattery.

But Billie knew that in one way, perhaps the most important way, Hayden did not deceive. For everyone knew what he was. However aloof and enigmatic he might seem at times, he was always *himself,* whereas she—she had not even been honest with the man she loved.

The June evening was hot and still. In an effort to catch the faintest of breezes, the Boehms had opened the windows throughout their house. Billie feared that once the company began to dance she might well expire, though she wore the thinnest of cool lawn gowns. Her sense of oppression had little to do with the heat. She had not been truthful with Hayden. She desperately wished to be free again. To be home and at liberty, to walk and ride for miles, or to sneak off to Braughton, to dream of David . . .

Attempting to school her features, she turned to the couple behind them. Her aunt Ephie had enjoyed the past two weeks. Hayden's access to the cream of the *ton* was unsurpassed, and Ephie had taken delighted advantage of the opportunity to visit the most exclusive of salons and parties. Hayden's friend Lord Knowles, at present escorting Ephie, often accompanied them as well, to ensure that neither lady should ever lack a turn on the dance floor, as Hayden's aversion to the pastime was quite renowned. Though Lord Knowles tended to talk a great deal, Billie found him a good-natured and attentive partner.

She spotted simpering May Sanders with Lord Grenby ahead on the stairs. The two had announced their engagement on the very day the *Times* had carried Hayden's spurious notice. As Billie caught Grenby's eye, she decided that he no longer looked sheepish. Grenby must think *her* as inconstant as he was. But he needn't look so very superior.

She hoped that she and Hayden would soon drop their sham betrothal, as it had served its purpose. Ronald Dumont had ceased to make a nuisance of himself. Indeed, she had heard he was off visiting his properties in Ireland. And as for Kit's debts—upon his return, Kit would certainly still owe. But word had come to Billie's ears that Hayden had won many of Kit's IOUs from Dumont, before that gentleman's departure. Billie supposed it marginally more comfortable to be outrageously in debt to one's neighbor than to a blackguard like

Dumont. Still, gentlemen were expected to honor their debts, lest they fail to be considered gentlemen.

Kit had written once from Brussels, a letter so entirely full of his own excitement and concerns that Billie wondered at herself for having wished to hear from him at all. Still, she had sent him a reply. By contrast, she had let ten days lapse before settling upon a suitable response to Lord David—a rudely unacceptable delay with any correspondent, but most particularly with the man one loved.

"A bit close, is it not?" Hayden asked her, perhaps noticing her frown.

Billie nodded. Hayden's friend, Lord Demarest, and Demarest's fiancée, Lady Constance, had joined their party and were eagerly exchanging news with Knowles. There had been word yesterday of battles south of Brussels. Bonaparte had bested the Prussians, and British residents in the city prepared to remove to Antwerp—to face a possible siege.

"This cannot all be happening again," Billie said, nervously working her fingers together in their soft kid gloves.

"Oh, it will all come right," Hayden told her.

"Why should you believe that?"

"Because David said so," he replied easily. Again Billie felt that sharp loss; she looked down to examine her gloves. "Time and numbers are against Bonaparte," Hayden continued. "He cannot fight us all. Eventually he must sue for peace."

"Only after many more have died."

Hayden did not respond. They were moving on past the stairs and into the spacious ballroom with the others. Billie could hear Mrs. Boehm, in her thickly Russian accent, addressing the Prince Regent, who had attended an earlier dinner. Ahead of them and to the side, everyone was bowing low or sweeping to the floor in a curtsy. Without even seeing the Regent, Billie followed suit. As the orchestra struck up the opening bars for a quadrille, Hayden tilted his head to her.

"I think I might suffer this one dance, my dear," he said,

extending a gloved hand, "if you would honor me. It avoids
that exhausting skippin' about."

She smiled and took his hand. But they had scarcely taken
their place in a set with Demarest and Lady Constance when a
hubbub arose from the street below. Billie thought the Corn
Law rioters must once again have invaded the West End. But
these cries were different; the crowd was *elated,* not angry. As
the music stopped, the Boehms' guests rushed to the wide windows, which, standing open, had carried all the noise from the
square. Billie could just catch sight of a speedy post chaise
escorted by a running, cheering throng. Two poles, with what
looked like flags and gilded statues at their ends, poked from
the carriage windows.

"What are those?" Billie asked Hayden. He stood next to
her, but, as he was at least half a foot taller, he had a much better view.

"Eagles," he said. "From Bonaparte's army." His voice was
strangely flat. Strangely, she thought, because all those pressing about them were so eager. The crowd in the street was ju-
bilant.

A mussed and dusty figure tumbled out of the carriage,
pulling the two "eagles" awkwardly along with him. Billie lost
sight of him; the crowd appeared to part only reluctantly as he
forged a path to the Boehms' front steps. There was a great
commotion from the hall, on the stairs. Within seconds the
waiting company had turned expectantly from the windows, to
observe a handsome but extremely untidy young officer enter
the ballroom.

"Percy," Hayden said softly. He grasped Billie's arm and
drew her closer to the visitor. "Percy" had dropped the poles
before the Regent and knelt now upon one knee.

"Victory, sir! Victory!"

Billie drew a sharp breath. The Prince Regent, after one second's relieved smile, gravely took some papers from Percy's
hand and retired without a word to a side room to read them.

While everyone else seemed struck immobile, Hayden moved quickly to Percy's side. Billie watched Hayden clap him on the shoulder and pump his hand. The younger man looked dazed. Others gathered around the messenger even as Hayden turned away.

"That's Henry Percy," Knowles whispered in her ear. "ADC to Wellington. Hayden knows him."

Hayden knew everyone. Billie watched his face as he returned to them.

"A victory south of Brussels, at Waterloo," he said. "Bonaparte bested and tearing back to France. And we must be off ahead of this lot." He was already steering Billie back through the now wildly exuberant crowd. "Thanks be, I had my carriage wait."

"But where are we off to, Hayden?" Demarest asked. "The Horse Guards?"

Hayden nodded sharply.

Billie thought she should be happy. Surely she *should* be happy. This was wonderful, astonishing news. But as they raced ahead of the other guests, down the stairs and out into the middle of the street, she felt only urgency—and dread.

"Why do we rush to the Horse Guards?" she asked.

"For the list," Demarest told her. "The first list of casualties."

Hayden's luxurious carriage easily held the six of them, but the air seemed as close and cloying as that in the Boehms' ballroom. Billie leaned her head back against the squabs and closed her eyes. She wished Hayden would not look so grim. Ephie was holding her hand. The trees in St. James's park blurred as the carriage sped past. When it stopped, Hayden leapt out, then checked—and turned to help Billie down. Billie had never seen him so quick and impatient. Whereas she—she felt numb.

"Come," Ephie said, taking her elbow. "We are some of the first here."

Indeed, they did not have to struggle to gain admittance. When Billie and Ephie passed the door, Hayden was already reading through pages. But he was still frowning. When he looked up and caught her gaze, she thought the frown deepened.

She forced herself to his side. Lord Demarest and Lord Knowles and the two other women were close behind her—like a wall, Billie thought, to help keep her upright.

Hayden handed her the list. "There is some mystery here," he said, pointing with a long forefinger at the list.

Billie's gaze fell to read: *Caswell, Christopher. Major, First Division, Guards/Coldstream. Wounded.*

"But this is wrong," she said.

"Yes. But it would seem your brother is still with us." Hayden took the list from her hands and perused it again before passing it on to Demarest and Knowles. "Miss Billie, there is no mention of David."

"Yes, I—yes, I saw."

"Not on the list as wounded or dead. Not on the list. And Percy knew nothing."

Around them, ladies were swooning, weeping. Lord Demarest was comforting Lady Constance, whose cousin, a cavalry officer, had been wounded. *Not on the list.* Should they believe, then, that David was well? She looked over Knowles' shoulder, to scan the many, many names—hundreds and hundreds of names. Athington—Charis' brother—dead? No, wounded. And there were too many other names. Someone beside her said most of Wellington's staff had been wounded or killed—all young, proud officers, some of whom Billie had just met this spring, gone, lost. And Kit wounded—how badly? She was still staring at the list, looking for a name she did not wish to find.

Lord Knowles was talking to Lady Constance, not with his usual easy flow of chatter but in a warm and coaxing manner. "This means nothing," he said reassuringly. Constance's eyes were red. "There is hope. You must rally. What are we, if not steadfast? We have certainly taken our blows. Why, you must know Demarest here is the last of his line. And George Gillen's two brothers went at Badajoz. I hardly knew my *pater,* lost at Aboukir Bay back in ninety-eight. You must have heard Percy's cry—"Victory!" Ah, what victory means to us all! 'Tis what has been taken from us in the winning that hurts so. Such decades of war! But think of all we have preserved. For coming years of peace! Your cousin will be well, Lady Cee. He might dance at your wedding!"

Billie had not realized she was standing with her eyes closed, listening, until she opened them in wonder. Lady Constance had stopped crying. And Billie looked to Knowles.

"I thank you, my lord," she told him. "I thank you most sincerely." Knowles looked surprised and pleased as he turned to her. "Without your aid," she admitted, "I fear I might have embarrassed myself."

"Never, Miss Caswell," he said gallantly. "And now I think—" He craned his neck to catch sight of Hayden returning to them. "Yes, I think we shall be off. Hayden's yacht is at Gravesend. Should cross within a day—"

"There is no word," Hayden said, interrupting him. He looked directly at Billie. "No word, good or bad. Do you understand me? This is a preliminary list. There were tens of thousands there, at Waterloo. It is a victory, but a disaster all the same. I shall leave before midnight. And, Knowles"—he looked to his friend—"will you venture over with me? Your French is passable."

Knowles beamed. "Certainly!"

Before Knowles could speak further, Hayden told Billie, "I must get you home." He attempted to lead her back toward the entrance. "This is a wretched business—"

"No," she said, balking. At the single, stubborn word he looked startled. "No, I will not go home. I am coming with you."

"But, Miss Billie, you cannot mean it! You do not under-stand. There is no room—"

"On your yacht, my lord? Or in Brussels? I should think an extra pair of hands would be welcome."

He tried to smile. "Yours—always. But the discomforts . . ."

"I would decide that for myself, Lord Hayden. I also have a brother who is wounded. And under the circumstances, we needn't continue to—to playact. Aunt Ephie needn't come."

"Aunt Ephie will most certainly come," Ephie inserted mildly. "As she also has a worthy pair of hands."

Hayden considered Billie with obvious resignation, but per-haps an equal measure of understanding. He sighed. "Then, ladies, let us collect your luggage and be off. Demarest?" he asked. "Will you join us?"

"I think I must be staying, Hayden. At least a day or two. If possible, I shall sail my own bark across later." He placed a consoling hand on the arm of Lady Constance, who still sniffled.

"I know Mama will not let me go," she choked, "even if—even if it *is* Freddy."

As their group left the Horse Guards', they shouldered their way out to the carriage. The place was now flooding with those running into the offices seeking information, some of them having arrived by foot from the Boehms'.

"Where is your brother this evening?" Hayden asked Billie. "We must tell him."

As Morty was dining at the Urquharts', just a few streets away from Ephie's town home, they stopped to see him first. Demarest set off on foot to escort Lady Constance around the corner. Billie and Hayden entered the Urquharts' and asked for Morty.

The Urquharts and their guests had just sat down to a late din-ner. After summoning an obviously irritated Morty into the hall, Hayden took him aside to explain their plans. As Billie waited impatiently at the door, she heard only Morty's "Kit!" All else was low, tense, and surprisingly brief. When Hayden walked on into the dining room to convey the news to those of his acquaintance at table, Morty came swiftly to Billie's side.

"Would you like me to go as well, Billie?" he asked. But she could tell he had little desire to do so.

"No. Ephie and I shall look to Kit, Morty. You mustn't leave Esther." She smiled at Esther, who had slipped out to join them in the hall. Behind her, the dining room had erupted in cheers.

"I am so sorry, Miss Billie," she said sweetly, "about Christopher."

"We will hope his injuries are not serious, Miss Esther," Billie assured her. "I must go now, Morty. We must leave at once. Lord Hayden told you Ephie comes with me?"

Morty nodded. "I should have insisted on it in any event," he said, sounding affronted. Looking over his shoulder at the entrance to the dining room, where Hayden was still engaged, he added disagreeably, "You really intend to *marry* that man?"

"Oh, Morty!" She did not know whether to laugh or to cry. "Can you truly be so insensible?"

As Morty looked nonplussed, Esther took her arm and led her to the door. "I shall explain it to him," she said softly. Hayden was returning promptly. "And I will pray you find your major."

Chapter Twelve

Billie had never before been at sea; she had only ever been aboard a simple skiff on calm lake waters. The crossing to Ostend left her bilious and green. As no one else on board was so affected, she had to bear the particular care and solicitude of her companions. That in itself would not have been difficult, had she not also had to endure Hayden's carefully blank face. He had warned her of the "discomforts" after all; they had not even reached Brussels, and she was already in distress. Despite her queasiness she stayed determinedly on deck, from their dawn departure on. Her one solace was that the crossing was brief.

She thought Hayden must regret consenting to her company. So she was surprised, once they were transferring to a slow canal barge from Ostend, when he troubled to relieve her mind.

"David has told me he never does well on the Channel crossing," he said simply, and Billie instantly viewed him with greater favor.

They moved on to Ghent, and at Ghent to a carriage pulled by a team that had seen better days. The driver told them that the army had requisitioned every serviceable horse—and that many thousands of them had been killed at Waterloo. The report silenced their already serious party. Billie was left to consider that this was the very same route that David had traveled in March. Indeed, she had his letter with her. If she had

160

replied to him promptly . . . if she had somehow managed to control Kit . . . *If, if!* As her anxiety mounted, she forced herself to pay attention to their surroundings.

What little she could see of the countryside in this last week of June was of farming—dairy cattle and vegetables and the occasional field of grain, with the consequent local farm vehicles. They were not the only travelers; there were also streams of people moving north, including one contingent of French prisoners.

Encountering any English troops, Hayden always inquired after David. No one had news of him. But much of the allied army, including the 52nd—Alan Athington's regiment and, initially, Kit's—had gone on to France, chasing Bonaparte.

Hayden was most generous with the ready, paying to send messengers to Hals, Enghien, and elsewhere asking after Guards officers. The response was always the same: casualties among all infantry officers from the battles at Quatre Bras and Waterloo had been appalling, perhaps as high as fifty percent. Many were as yet "unrecovered." Swallowing her dismay, Billie chose to believe they would soon learn something of import at Brussels.

But the minute they passed through the ancient walls of the city, she wished she had not insisted on coming. For the town was in great confusion—hot, steamy, and malodorous with the crowded, wounded, and unwashed. The sidewalks were still covered with straw, where great numbers of wounded men, given no other shelter, had lain for days. Hayden told her it had taken three days to collect the allied wounded from the battlefield; many of the French wounded had had to await help even longer. The terrible situation for such men soon roused Billie's sympathies rather than her shock. Amid that mass of suffering she was more determined than ever to find Kit and David and to render whatever assistance she might.

Hayden had procured them two rooms—seemingly the last available—on the Rue de la Madeleine, at l'Hotel d'Angleterre.

As most of the English community seemed to be housed near the Royal Palace and the park, he assured Billie they would soon be in close communication with those who would have word of their brothers.

Billie and Ephie settled into their tiny room with the maid, Simms, and washed some of the travel dirt from their faces and hands. They would have to share the bed, with Simms on the trestle, as all available mattresses and bedding had been surrendered to the care of the wounded. The circumstances were indeed dire.

"You boasted of your capable hands, lass," Ephie said mildly as they met each others' glances. "We are not likely to remain untested."

"I shall do what I can, Ephie," Billie said, though the extent of the problems overwhelmed her. "But first I should just like . . . that is, I need to *know.*"

Ephie nodded as they set out to join Hayden and Knowles to walk the few blocks to the house the Athingtons had leased so close to the park. Though the bright sun beat hotly outside, the curtains were shut; the front hall was dark and the air too close. Billie heard a groan from a salon to her right; the footman told them that the Athingtons were housing half a dozen other wounded soldiers in their lower rooms.

Mr. Athington, advancing from down the hall, bowed to Hayden.

"My lord, I had your note," he said, acknowledging the rest of them with nods. "Do come on back and see Alan. He is— he is doing well." And they followed him into a back parlor, which seemed airier than the rest of the house.

Charis and her mother, who had been sitting on opposite sides of the single bed, rose rather stiffly as their visitors entered. But Billie was not in the mood for ceremony.

"Charis!" she said, moving forward to kiss the beauty on the cheek. Charis would always look lovely, but just now her face was anguished.

"Miss—Miss Billie," she gulped. "So good of you to—Oh!" she burst out, her celebrated composure snapping in a flood of tears. "They do hope to spare his arm!"

Billie helped her to sit. She glanced at Alan Athington, who lay upon the bed. Whatever pain or worries he had, his gaze was alert and bright.

"Miss Caswell, you mustn't mind m'sister. She is bein' a goose. How d'you do, Hayden? Knowles. Miss Caswell—"

"Athington," Hayden said, "we would not have troubled you—"

"Not at all! Glad of the company. There are so many of us bedridden, there are too few to make calls!" He seemed to find this worthy of a laugh. Billie thought his color healthy, though he looked to have lost weight. "I shall be laid up here some time. Might as well make the best of it. And there are too many grim faces about. I'll tell you, Hayden, my greatest pain at the moment is not bein' able to march on Paris with the Fifty-second!"

"So speaks the British infantry." Hayden bowed deeply to him. "I commend you, Lieutenant."

Athington blushed. "Shouldn't even have been *here* without your brother, Hayden. Demmed—demmed fine thing he did."

"Oh, we can never repay him!" Charis added, with such a generous look that Billie had to fight a most uncharitable thought.

"I am sure he would not think of it, Miss Athington," Hayden said. "But do tell us, when did you last see him?"

"See him?" Charis looked confused. "Why, we have not seen him at all. Has he not gone on to Paris with the Duke of Wellington?"

As Hayden frowned, Billie tried to tamp down the anxiety that had been growing for days. She had convinced herself there would be word from one of Hayden's many messengers, that there would be news once they reached Brussels, that the

Athingtons would surely know. But Hayden's frown made her shiver.

"Do tell us how you came here," Knowles asked Athington, "and how you do?"

So Alan Athington relayed the tale of his rescue, which lent Billie some minimal comfort, although David's risk had equaled his bravery.

"I doubt I should have survived at all without his aid," Athington said. "And certainly not with the use of my limbs. Charis moans about this ruddy arm, but even that's nothing compared to others. . . ." He went on, much too explicitly. Billie was thankful when Hayden interrupted, perhaps noticing—as Billie did—the Athington ladies' white faces.

"Have you seen anything further of Barton, then?"

"No. Though that reminds me . . . Mama, open the drawer there, would you please?" And Mrs. Athington slid open a nightstand drawer to pull out a watch. She passed it to Hayden.

"It's Trent's," Athington said. "Barton didn't want it on 'im, apparently. Said he was returning to the line to find the major, and there were too many rough folk about robbing and Lord knows what else. Didn't have to sell it after all, what?" And again evidencing good spirits, Athington laughed.

Hayden was rubbing the old gold in one hand.

"Have you heard anything of my brother, Lieutenant?" Billie asked. "Of Kit?"

"*I* haven't. But Charis has, haven't you, old girl?"

Charis clearly attempted a smile, though it was apparent that she did not much care for being termed "old girl."

"I heard from the Harradays, across the square, that they'd seen him in hospital with their son—oh, three days ago. But he was talking then about running off after the army to France. I—I fear I have no news of his injuries, Miss Billie. I have not left this house."

"You needn't apologize, Miss Athington. I would never have expected it." She now found it difficult to sit politely.

The men made some few further comments on the battle and their shared acquaintance. Though the victory had been decisive, though word had come of Bonaparte's abdication just days before, the toll had been ghastly for both sides. The battle site, Mr. Athington relayed, was a place of horror—fifteen thousand allied soldiers dead, with a third of all the British forces lost and at least as many French and horses.

Abruptly, and to Billie's relief, Hayden said, "We must be getting on. Athington, I see your eyes startin' to close upon me. I cannot suffer it in any man."

"No, indeed, Hayden," the lieutenant managed wearily. His parents thanked them as they made their way to the door. Mr. Athington offered them the use of his open carriage with, he apologized, a very old team. The army had requisitioned his best cattle in May. Yet the carriage had been usefully employed in ferrying the wounded for four days the previous week.

Charis, perhaps in her own way now "recovered," stared rather pointedly at Billie's ringless left hand and then glanced quickly through her lashes up at Hayden.

"Am I to wish you happy, then, Miss Caswell?" she asked.

"I hope so, Miss Athington. I truly hope so."

As they turned away from the Athingtons' home, Billie heard Hayden mutter ominously, "And now for Kit Caswell."

They walked on in the wilting heat, discussing the brave spirits of Alan Athington and his description of David Trent's selfless action. Billie felt little desire to see the battlefield or the Hougoumont farm. She was indescribably discouraged. But if she must . . .

"Billie dear," Ephie asked her, "Should you like a rest first?" But Billie denied any need for a break. Ephie also disclaimed any interest in returning to the hotel. Both of them seemed determined to deprive Lord Hayden of reason to regret their company.

The state of the city was appalling. Not only private houses but churches as well had been turned into hospitals, but this generosity had scarcely alleviated the magnitude of misery. The Athingtons had told them that, during the first days after the battle, the people of Brussels had sent out thirty wagons daily to collect the wounded. Those casualties who could walk or ride had made their own way into town. And almost all the wounded had borne further injuries or some degree of suffering from exposure—from being stripped not only of valuables and mementos but often as well of the simplest of clothing. Brussels, Billie realized, had been compelled to confront the needs of an unanticipated, additional population within its medieval gates, resulting in much heartache and disorder.

At the allied hospital she almost hesitated to step in. Hayden kept them at a tiny office and read through the names.

"Christopher is no longer here," he said in obvious frustration, and in response to her mute query added, "and David never was." He suggested they return to the hotel for some rest and dinner. They were still in their traveling clothes from early that morning. Hayden repeated that he had left inquiries in every corner of the city.

"But Barton," Billie said as they retraced their steps toward the park, "Lord David's batman—where can he be?"

"One hopes—with David," Hayden replied. And they parted silently for their rooms.

Billie and Ephie had changed for dinner and were about to go down when Simms answered a knock at the door. Beyond it, leaning partly upon crutches, was Kit.

"Kit!" Billie moved to him at once, relieved of at least one worry. Though thankful, she knew she might have been happier still.

"'Allo, Billie, Auntie." He attempted a smile. "You might touch me, you know—I won't break!"

"You look—you *look* as though you might," Billie said.

"Oh, but I cannot—I've already broken so much else!" Yet he sounded cheerful enough. He tolerated their kisses, then settled with some care into their single upholstered chair. "Hayden thought I ought to come up and see you at once, to set your minds at ease. I've been in lodgings with several others up at the Namur gate, where Hayden's message reached us." His smile was still the same. Billie wondered how a man could suffer through Waterloo and not change one whit.

"You must tell us, Christopher," Ephie said at her most forbearing, "how you come to be sporting crutches."

"I am lucky to be sporting anything at all, Auntie—or so I've been told." He went on to relate how he'd been knocked from his horse, broken several ribs and his ankle, been crushed and trampled repeatedly, but never struck by musket fire or shells. The surgeon expected he would recover fully, though they would continue to watch him for signs of internal injuries. He did not know if he would limp. How he had come to be so far to the rear, strapped upon Major Trent's horse, he hadn't a clue.

"He must've put me there, though I've no memory of it. We must have been at the line. I did hear some Frenchman yelling. But all else is a blur."

"Did you tell Hayden this?" Billie asked.

"Oh, yes. And Barton's down with him now."

"Barton?"

"Trent's batman. He found me two days ago. After he found the horse. Incendio, I think he called 'im. And Barton sent a letter off to Hayden. But of course, all of you were already on your way here—"

"Barton's not with Lord David."

Kit gave her an odd look. "I've just told you, the man's downstairs. We've been invited to dinner. Then I shall stop to see Athington and must work my way back to old General Smallwood somehow, though this *reporting* right and left does tire—"

"Everything 'tires' for you, Kit," Billie said in sudden frustration. "You left your regiment without leave."

"Well, yes. I imagine it appears I pulled a bit of a leg bail, given the debts. But they'll be paid, Billie—you shall see. And who can blame me for coming on here? Smallwood encouraged me. And, given the victory, I 'spect all will be forgiven at home. There's already talk about pension payments and awards and holidays—"

Billie sat down on the arm of his chair, interrupting his casual list of extravagant expectations. "You really remember nothing of how you came to be on David's horse?"

"No, Billie. As I told Hayden, I was quite without my senses. I even had his coat about me, but I don't recall it at all."

"Yet he clearly assured your safety."

"I s'pose."

At that Billie jumped up from his chair. "You are quite abominable, Kit Caswell! Lord David saved your life, and you still resent him!"

Kit looked suddenly sullen. "I don't much care to be in debt to 'im," he muttered.

"In debt to him? You don't mind being in debt to everyone else!"

Kit struggled to rise from the chair. Watching him, Billie felt instantly contrite. But he always made her feel so, and to no good end.

"How long have you been perfect?" he asked crossly. "Has the idea of becoming a marchioness gone to your head?"

"I am not 'perfect,' Kit. You know I do not think of myself so. And I shall never be a marchioness."

"Then what's all this business with Hayden? I thought—"

"I doubt you did think, Kit! I wouldn't be engaged to Hayden were it not for you. If you hadn't been so—so *rolled up* by Dumont, 'twould never have been necessary! You must know the engagement was to keep Dumont from seeking my portion. And now I believe David would not be missing if it weren't for you—running off and hoaxing, *wheedling* your way where you'd no business to be! He gave his horse to you, he gave his coat to you, and possibly—possibly his *life*! If anything—if something has happened to him, I shall never forgive you!" Billie could scarcely breathe. Though all of it was the truth, she suspected it should not have been said.

There was a long silence in their tiny room. Then Kit said distantly, "Well, that's clear enough." He looked then so pale and thin, leaning on his crutches, that Billie almost apologized. But Ephie saved her from spoiling her own victory.

"Shall we go on down to dinner? Everyone seems a bit peckish."

Ephie aided a hobbling Kit as they made their way to a table in the dining room. There were no private parlors; they had all been lent out as rooms. At the side of the table Hayden introduced Barton, a large, open-featured man of perhaps forty, who had been invited to join their dinner group.

Billie reached to shake Barton's hand. "I must thank you for all you have done, for Lieutenant Athington and my brother."

"That's all right, miss."

"Is Major Trent's horse doing well?"

"Oh, nothing troubles Incendio, miss. He'll be all to rights once the major's back."

Would it were so, Billie thought, taking her seat. She did not recall when she had last eaten, but she had no appetite now.

The others did not appear to share her listlessness. Neither was the table silent. Lord Knowles kept up his usual discourse, with sustaining additions from Ephie and Kit. Hayden refrained from speaking much, though the occasional hotel guest, seeing him, would stop by at their exposed table to greet him. Barton did not speak at all, until at one point Kit addressed her as "Billie."

"Ah—*you're* 'Billie,' then!" Barton exclaimed. He said nothing more but stole glances at her as he ate. When she caught him at it, he smiled.

As the meal ended, Hayden surveyed the table.

"We have no place to which to retire. So regrettably we must share our news here. Mr. Barton has been kind enough to

join us." Hayden inclined his head to Barton at the opposite
end of the table. "So I will ask him to relay to the rest of you
what he told me before dinner."

That the Marquis of Hayden should have requested his
brother's batman, a servant, to speak so, was a measure of his
concern. But Barton certainly did not appear overwhelmed by
the unusual invitation. He thanked Hayden, then spoke of the
last time he had seen the major, how he had later come upon
Incendio and Kit, and his efforts to quiz survivors of the battle
regarding the major's whereabouts.

"So you see, genelmen an' ladies, as near as I can tell, he
never made it back down to the farm, where he was to meet
me. And the last person rememberin' speakin' to 'im was an
officer of the *Hanovrins*. So, if he did not move on with the
advance—and I cannot think as he would've, havin' mentioned
the farm—he must have stayed somewheres on the slope behind it. The duke—that's Lord Wellington—demanded lists
last week before he went on to Paris—of all the wounded an'
those in hospital. And the officers was asked to list deserters.
A stickler the duke was about it too! And the major weren't on
any of those lists."

"He is dead, then," Billie said flatly. Even as she said it, she
did not feel it. But she spoke to convince herself.

Hayden regarded her steadily. "It is what we dread, Miss
Billie. And thus, in this unfortunate circumstance, it appears
the more likely. But we must rely on facts, not our fears, for
the truth of it. Barton assures me that he covered the ground,
looking among the dead. . . ."

"They did have to bury many where they lay, my lord," Barton inserted, at which Billie felt as though she had again
crossed the Channel.

Hayden glanced swiftly at her, then asserted, "Those cases
were quite different, though, weren't they, Barton? Now—"
He looked to the others. "We have a horse, a coat, a watch, but
no Major Trent. Barton last spoke with him just prior to the

confrontation with the French Imperial Guard. However mad David might appear in the usual course, he is a most disciplined officer. He is unlikely to have joined the allied advance rashly and without a weapon, though we cannot discount that he might have salvaged one. His last known action was to aid Mr. Caswell, who remembers nothing."

"Except the Frenchman yelling," Kit put in petulantly.

"But the French cannot have been upon you yet, else David would never have spared the time for such elaborate care— even for you, Mr. Caswell. You must have imagined the Frenchman."

"I know a Frenchie when I hear one!"

As Billie winced at the term, Hayden granted Kit one singularly intent look, then smoothly opened a palm to Knowles. "Knowles, my friend, would you do me the honor and kindly educate our young guest?"

"What? Oh! Delighted." And Knowles, who looked so indisputably English, launched upon such a stream of perfect French that Kit's jaw dropped.

Barton laughed. "The major was always quick with the 'parleyvous' as well, my lord," he said.

At that, Billie's memory of David was so intense as to be painful. Had he been quick with the 'parleyvous,' as Barton said? She supposed so. He had ever been quick. And he spoke French with his lovely *grand-mère.* . . .

She drew a sharp, comprehending breath as she leaned toward Hayden.

"My lord," she said urgently. "Your *grand-mère* told me he will speak what he hears, habitually, without thought. We have been looking in the wrong army." And by the light in his gaze, she knew that Hayden understood her.

Chapter Thirteen

They found new inspiration and energy. The next morning, while Hayden, Knowles, and Barton fanned out across the countryside in search of a "French" David, Billie visited the hospital for the wounded French prisoners in Brussels. The good ladies of the city were engaged in ministering to all the luckless survivors of Waterloo, an endeavor that seemed, at least to Billie, to require not only great fortitude but great quantities of bandages for dressing wounds. The production of lint required most of their time.

Volunteering to dispense refreshments to the patients, Billie viewed every man there but failed to find the one man she sought. And on her rounds she found it easier not to focus on the maladies of any particular soldier, to concentrate solely on her task, for some of the individual cases were heartbreaking.

Hayden returned late that night with the news that, in the confused withdrawal toward Paris, the few prisoners the French had taken, most of them Prussian, had managed to escape. The French were said to have been in such disarray that they'd had difficulties looking even to themselves.

This news left the possibility that David might have been wounded and collected by a local resident, either someone who had not had the means to transport him into the city or, perhaps, a sympathizer with Bonaparte—a partisan who intended to see French soldiers returned to France. David had written of such sympathies among the country folk. But if he

172

had been unable to leave within a week, whatever injuries he had sustained must be severe indeed.

On the second day, Hayden borrowed Mr. Athington's team. Hayden, Knowles, Billie, and Ephie drove out along the road toward Nivelles, in the southwest, where Wellington had moved his army the day after Waterloo. Barton took Incendio out separately, to circle toward Enghien, where David had been billeted before the battle.

" 'Tis possible someone picked 'im up and could not easily bring him on into town," Hayden said, managing to coax Athington's team temporarily to a trot. They skirted the battlefield, which Billie had no wish to see—the stories she had heard over the past two days had been sufficiently harrowing. The image of a muddy plain, thick with the dead, had taken root in her mind; she wondered whether a battleground took as long as its combatants to heal. As their party passed, they found that the stench of gunpowder, fire, and smolder lingered. Even the farms to the west of the site showed evidence of upheaval—the flattened fields of rye, crushed hedges and gardens, and abandoned, broken vehicles all spoke of the recent chaos.

They had been traveling more than two hours out of town, the ladies with their parasols spread wide against the hot sun, and the open carriage—little more than a wagon—grew increasingly dusty, for the road was only partially cobbled and the remainder dry earth and ruts. Billie conceded that Hayden was certainly a fine driver, not only to elicit so much from such a team, but to make the ride tolerable. To spare the horses, they stopped frequently at farmhouses nearest the road, to show *grand-mère*'s locket miniature of David and make inquiries. Knowles, whose facility with the language was so extraordinary, was tasked with asking after any guests in the vicinity. Billie suspected that Hayden's French was almost as good, but for some reason he preferred not to speak it.

In this plodding and discouraging manner, they moved

perhaps two miles beyond the battlefield, following the sun, which had slipped into a hot afternoon blaze. They resorted to their canteens more than once.

"Rather a shocking business for these farmers," Knowles remarked. "Imagine the ill fortune to have just this spot chosen for such a contest—and their year's crops just starting to thrive."

"And then to have their emperor bested," Hayden added dryly.

"Not all, Hayden. Not all! Why, some have told me they always supported the allies."

"Oh, I am sure they do—now."

"Not everything is politics, Lord Hayden," Ephie said with spirit. "No doubt the state of their stomachs will convince them of much."

"You have the way of it, Miss Caswell," Knowles affirmed. "Once they have a few good years of harvests, these farmers will forget any indignities."

"One does not easily surrender a generation of glory," Hayden said. "Why do you think Bonaparte received the welcome he did in March?"

"Well, as to that—" But Knowles abruptly ceased talking, because as they crested a slight rise in the road, they looked down upon a trampled farmstead. And standing at its rickety gate, with his left arm in a sling and the other holding a package from which a crust of bread protruded, Lord David was apparently taking leave of a local farming couple.

Hayden halted the team. As the Belgian pair scurried back into their home, David looked the few hundred feet up the road toward their wagon. To their astonishment, he turned his back upon them and calmly started to walk in the opposite direction.

Billie wanted to scream. How dare he—after all of this! Her fists clenched, but when she glanced toward Hayden, his face was impassive. Billie thought he briefly shook his head.

"Goodness!" Ephie exclaimed. "Isn't that Lord David there ahead of us? Why do you not—"

"Beg pardon, ma'am," Hayden interrupted. "I should prefer to see what he is about." And as they drove on past the farmhouse and yard, his gaze surveyed both most minutely.

Billie could not take her attention from David, walking along ahead of them. He was booted but without a coat or hat. His dark hair looked longer and shone in the sun. He was much thinner, even rangy, which somehow made his shoulders appear even broader. His shirt and breeches were stained and torn. The rude sling tied in a knot at his nape, and the arm—*what was wrong with his arm*? Billie thought he did not walk briskly. *But he was walking. He was whole. He was safe.*

Her relief was physical. Gratitude made her tremble. As their carriage came closer, she willed David to stop. When he did, and turned to face the road, Billie felt his gaze as a caress.

The carriage pulled up beside him, and David smiled—a wide and beautiful smile that erased what must have been lines of pain from his pale face. For a moment he looked up at Billie, and from her height on the wagon seat, she looked down upon him. She thought the warmth in his eyes something wonderful. Then his glance sought out the other occupants of the carriage. He raised his package-laden right arm to point down the road before them, as though giving them direction.

"If you would, Myles," he said, and his voice delighted her, "just drive on up over this next rise, so that I might avoid being shot as a spy." Again his gaze returned to her, his face alight with his smile—so much so that, despite the shock of his words, she could not heed him with any seriousness. Quickly she slipped from her seat and down into the dusty roadway, to block his body with her own.

"Do stop playing, David," Hayden said, "and climb up here with us. You see Miss Billie dares to protect you."

"I see that," David said softly. He was looking not at Hayden but at her. "She is very brave."

" 'Tis foolish," she breathed. His gaze mesmerized her. "As you've told me before."

"Perhaps both, Billie dear, as I am fairly certain a musket is pointed at your back. My former benefactor has questionable aim and a rusty weapon, but I should hate to have him accidentally shoot Lord Knowles."

"I say, David! That's awfully good of you. . . ." And Knowles was still elaborating as David quickly tossed him the package before swinging Billie up into the wagon with his still-strong right arm. He was following up behind her as Hayden sprang the team. The ancient animals actually thundered ahead for fifty yards.

Billie had to content herself with being jolted up against David's side. As this was his injured arm, she could not think it equally agreeable to him. But still she sat as close as she could, and he did not protest.

"I must be grateful to them," he explained, his voice unsteady as the wagon bounced, "to the Beaulieus—whatever their aim in rescuing me. They troubled to house two others, French officers from horse artillery. I improvised and claimed to be one of my French opponents—of Colonel Cubières's troops at the farm. But I fear they began to suspect that I was one of the reviled English. Too much staring at my best boots—by Hobbs you know, Myles." And Billie glanced at his dulled and dirty boots. "Had they been Beaulieu's size . . . Well! I knew I had to convince them I was returning to service or else resign myself to slow poisoning. Tell me—pleased as I am to see you—how do you all come to be here? Hasn't Boney closed the roads?"

The question was greeted with such a profound silence that David's eyebrows rose.

"You mean you do not know"—Hayden's voice cracked—"that Wellington was victorious? That you *won*?"

Billie could feel David's stillness. She could also feel the constraint of being denied even the clasp of his hand.

"That old fox!" he fumed. "Beaulieu and his invincible Bonaparte! He's been feeding us the opposite—that the French had a great victory, that Bonaparte is in Brussels and collecting more troops at the border. I shall go back and pummel him!"

"How can you look so happy, then," Hayden demanded, "thinking that you'd lost?" At David's slow grin, Hayden pointedly turned his attention to the road.

"Monsieur Beaulieu thought you French," Billie said, forcing the words. She recalled with some impatience that David had never before been disinclined to kiss her. "Perhaps he only meant to buoy your spirits. Yours and the other two men."

"You are too kind to him, Miss Billie." David's close attention warmed her like sunlight. "The man was out looting early. And you did not see the gleam in his eye! Tell me—the Imperial Guard—defeated?" And David listened as the other three narrated what they had heard: of Bonaparte's vaunted guard falling into confusion, how the French had broken and run, how Wellington had signaled a general advance at dusk. The Prussians had since poured into France on a vengeful rampage, and Wellington was proceeding to Paris, having passed along this very road.

"He will not let up," David said with satisfaction. Again looking down at Billie, he asked seriously, "What of your brother?"

"Kit does very well, thanks to you. He is walking, though he contends with crutches."

"And Lieutenant Athington?"

"Less well. He is cheerful, though still bedridden. He speaks of frustration at not going on to Paris. Unfortunately, he may lose his arm."

"I am sorry to hear it. His sister has my sympathies."

Billie did not know how to respond.

"What of your own arm?" Hayden asked abruptly. "Shall you keep it?"

"Oh, I hope so, Myles, as it's my best boxing arm." He sent

Hayden a narrow glance. "'Tis my shoulder that's injured. Fortunately, Madame Beaulieu's cousin, professing some medical training, stopped by for a meal on his way to Brussels. He removed a musket ball within that first day and left Madame enough laudanum to dose me into the next decade—at least, I fear I shall be reeling that long. Apparently I also suffered shock from a spent shell, though I've no memory of it. The shame is that Madame was a wonderful chef. Aromas from her kitchen kept me half wild with expectation. But the laudanum deprived me of appetite as well as pain. I doubt they'd have fed us much in any event, though the French officers endeavored to pay them. . . . That's her bread you're holding there, Knowles."

Knowles promptly broke off a piece and proffered it to Ephie, who pronounced it delicious.

"'Tis delightful to have a picnic here in the country, David," Hayden remarked. "But might I trouble to inquire—where we are goin'?"

Billie felt David's attention to her profile and turned to look fully at him.

"Where were you going before you came upon me?" he asked, though he looked only at her.

"'Came upon' you!" Ephie protested. "Surely you know we've been searching for you?"

"Have you?" His gaze held Billie's captive. "Am I to call you 'sister,' then?" he asked softly.

"You are precipitant," Hayden drawled. "The *Times*' announcement is scarcely out."

"How curious, Myles. Here I thought *you* precipitant." He did not appear amused as he looked across at Hayden. "You must know it's a demnable thing to hear in the midst of a war."

"I'd have thought it demnable to hear at any point. But you must know that it is nonsense."

"Fine. Then why?"

"Dumont."

"Ah!" He looked down at her then, his face very close, and suggested, "You and I are fond of carriage rides, are we not?"

At the reminder of the New Year, Billie blushed. She was, she knew, exceedingly fond of *him*. But she could not tell him so just yet—not within hearing of the others, who seemed to have endless questions. She did convince herself that David leaned immeasurably closer, that his left boot pressed against her skirts, and this time she did not object.

They turned at the next crossroads and found their way as quickly as possible back toward the north and east, speaking all the while of Waterloo, of men lost and saved, of actions wise and less so, and at last of Hougoumont. As they shared information, David's mood became increasingly grave. Billie wished to touch him; she wished to be only with him. She had to concentrate on sitting straight on the rickety wagon seat.

"Wellington's said that if Hougoumont had not held," Knowles prompted, "there would not have been a victory."

"I would not dare dispute him," David said. "Though every effort counted. 'Tis certain we fought as though that were the case. 'Twas a very bitter business, indeed. I was never as weary in my life!" He paused. "Someday I must find that boy."

"What boy?" Billie asked.

"Why, Guillaume, my little savior. I called him Billie." His glance indulged her. "He stayed with me that first night and ran to the Beaulieus' wagon to have them collect me before dawn. They had some other French wounded they placed with friendly families, lest they be taken prisoner. The Beaulieus' farm had served as a staging area for French artillery the day before battle. Beaulieu was, as I said, out to see what he might gather; the boy must have triggered some itch of sympathy, or else Beaulieu hoped my teeth were of marketable ivory!" David smiled broadly, displaying them. "Guillaume stayed with us only a day, but long enough, apparently, to convince them I was French. That boy had a head on him! I was not in my right senses, you understand. He must have departed soon after Wellington passed through to Nivelles. Little Guillaume could not have been more than twelve."

"Twelve! That is terribly young to be at war!"

"There is no good age, Miss Billie. Guillaume's only weapon was a drum. And as I remember it, you must have been about twelve when you decided to shoot your neighbor."

At that she stayed silent. She thought she heard Ephie titter behind her.

When they entered Brussels the sun had just set. At the hotel, Barton met them with joy. He and Hayden and Knowles spirited David off to the gentlemen's single room, to claim a wash and a coat. Billie felt in need of considerable repair herself. She had been sitting for some hours next to David in the wagon, and in all that time she had said very little. But she had felt much. She knew her own anxiously awaited interview was at hand.

Ephie was silent as they changed for dinner, but Billie found her aunt's many assessing glances annoying. "Do say what you wish to say, Auntie," she challenged at last.

"I doubt that I need say anything, Billie. When one is given a second chance—or, no, I believe it is a *third* chance—one is usually aware of the fact."

"Yes, one usually is, Ephie."

And Ephie, smiling in satisfaction, preceded her downstairs.

In the dining room, David stood alone at the end of their table. As it was still early, very few guests were down. Billie noticed that he now wore a dress coat, but the substitution for his uniform scarcely signified; the coat suited him equally well.

"This is Hayden's," he told her, noticing the direction of her gaze. "In the usual course, I am too stout for his wardrobe. I must commend him for his discipline in diet."

Billie suspected her smile was rather wan.

"You will regain your health quickly, I am certain, Major,"

Ephie said brightly, but her own smile soon slid into a frown as she glanced about her. "Do forgive me. I seem to have left my reticule upstairs. I shall be back directly." At once she turned and left them.

David drew out a chair and offered it to Billie. As she sat down, he took the seat nearest her. She noticed that his rough muslin sling had been replaced by one of crisp white linen.

"Barton appears to be a most attentive batman," she remarked.

"Indeed. Between Barton and Hayden's man, Phipps, I am very well set up. But I must be back in uniform, and on duty, as soon as possible. Barton has gone for my trunk just now."

"But you are wounded!"

He smiled. "I am also a commissioned officer, in an army at war. I have not been given my *congé,* Miss Billie. I am absent without leave—a malingerer. My superiors have every right to have me flogged."

"You jest with me," she said sharply. "Surely, under the circumstances—"

"Yes," he agreed, and Billie was suddenly aware of how close he sat, "the circumstances are extraordinary." His eyes looked very blue in his pale face. "I could use another day's rest."

"A day!"

"It has been an exhausting time, you'll agree," he said, choosing to misunderstand her, "and one that has brought almost as much tragedy as joy. So many good men, so many friends are gone. . . ." He paused, his gaze darkening. "Well, I must write letters—now—tonight."

"I should like to hear," she offered softly, "when you wish to speak of it."

"And I should like to tell you—no doubt to the point you grow weary." He grinned, which erased the sober set of his features. "But first, I am glad to have this moment alone with you—Billie."

She wished they were not so publicly situated; she wished they were not seated here in such a fashion, when she could think only of the dark stairwell in her aunt's London home. The hotel's guests, though understandably somber, tended to be loud in their efforts at exchanging news.

"You never told your father that you'd thrown me over," he continued, his gaze steady on hers. "Hayden says Sir Moreton was shocked by the sudden . . . transfer of your affections." He tapped the fingers of his right hand upon the table. "Why did you not tell your father?"

"You were away. It hardly seemed to matter. I had no interest in anyone else. What difference could it have made?" She thought her own voice a bit too strident.

"You made no response to my letter. Because of the business with Hayden?"

"I am very sorry for that, indeed. I meant to respond. But I thought I would have more time. I had no expectation that you would be called to action when you were."

"Nor had we."

"But it was no excuse. Not after your perfectly fine letter. I ask your forgiveness." He smiled but did not comment, and Billie glanced over her shoulder at the increasingly crowded dining room. "This is dreadful," she said, dismayed. "I wish we were not here!"

David shrugged. " 'Tis where we happen to be. Don't think on it. Or better yet, recall your stand at the Sanderses' that evening, and resolve to weather it. The audience is nothing." In his gaze she read the instant that he recalled their New Year's kiss. "In fact, I am tempted," he hinted mildly, "to repeat myself—with a most public display." Though his blue gaze entranced her, though she had wanted to kiss him all afternoon, she shook her head. Ephie would be back.

"Ours is not a simple affair, is it, Billie?"

"No . . ."

"And yet, it might have been. Very. We might even have

been married months ago. And then I doubt we should even have been here in Brussels."

" 'The world is too much with us,' " she quoted softly.

He smiled. "Perhaps now we might set it aside? I've told Hayden," he added firmly, "that you've cried off."

"Shall I call you presumptuous?"

"You might call me whatever you wish, my dear. But a woman should not look at a man as you look at me—then marry another."

"You *are* presumptuous!" But she could not help her own smile.

He reached inside his waistcoat pocket. Pulling forth his fist, he opened his palm to display two items—a musket ball and a small, sharp arrowhead. The latter looked like what it had been—a child's deadly toy. Billie's lips parted as she glanced first at the arrowhead and then up into David's face.

"Years ago," he said, "my father's surgeon dared not remove it. The Beaulieus' quack cousin had no such qualms. I suspect he cared less for my life." As Billie reached to touch the items, his warm fingers closed on hers. "Oddly, once the token was out, I knew I should never be free of it. And the ball could not harm a heart already lost—to you, Billie Caswell."

She could not seem to draw breath.

" 'Tis why I shot at you," she choked out.

"Little savage." His hand tightened upon hers. "You might have killed me."

"Are you—are you in much pain now?"

He shook his head. Billie knew that their close *tête-à-tête,* the touch of their hands, drew fascinated attention in the busy dining room.

"Ephie has been an unconscionably long time. . . ." she said.

"I cannot agree. Your aunt is like the very finest officers, hanging about only when one needs them."

"You mean that she purposely stays away?"

"I believe so." He leaned closer. "Billie, if I must go on to Paris, will you wait for me?"

"To Paris?" She shook her head. "No."

"Ah!" He frowned, but the clasp of his hand did not ease. "Have I misunderstood, then? When you did not write—"

"I cannot bear all the waiting," she said in a rush. "I have waited all spring. I will not do it! *You* would not suffer it. Why should I?"

His features relaxed. "I certainly will not suffer it! Which is why Hayden has gone for the bishop." At her questioning gaze, he added, "He is very good at this sort of arrangement."

"The—bishop?"

David laughed. "One certainly hopes so! But no, I meant that Hayden has done this before—hurried a wedding along. Do you recall, dearest, the tune you played for me at the New Year? The 'Soldier's Delight'? I told you that it referred to home. I have determined that *you* are my home, Billie. My home, and my happiness. I would have you with me always." His clasp tightened.

Conversation in the rest of the room had grown to an enveloping hum. Billie now scarcely noticed the noise. Having waited so long, she saw only David.

"There is a chance," he added, "that I might take a regiment out to India. If I do, shall we have your brother Kit along with us?"

The offer dazed her. "You would do that? For him?"

"I would do it for you."

As she moved to place her trembling right palm atop their clasped hands, he startled her by abruptly withdrawing his own. Sliding from his chair, he knelt on one knee before her.

The dining room instantly hushed.

"Billie—*querida,*" he urged, "would you do me the very great honor?"

She held his intent gaze as she rose. "I fear you will miss your dinner, Major."

"I am not hungry."

"Then . . . there is a waning moon tonight." She fought a smile. Memories of Ephie's stairwell ruled her mind. "It is quite dark out-of-doors. I would welcome your escort." She extended both hands to help him up.

As he stood, his look held laughter. "Brave Billie," he said, pulling her close, "you will have to marry me now."

And they stepped together into the warm June night.